The Eridanos Library

Ernst Jünger

A DANGEROUS
ENCOUNTER

Translated from the German by
HILARY BARR

The Eridanos Library
MARSILIO PUBLISHERS

Original German title *Eine gefährliche Begegnung*

The publication of this book was made possible in part through
a generous grant from InterNationes

ISBN: 0-941419-37-1
LC 92-62372

First edition

MANUFACTURED IN THE UNITED STATES OF AMERICA

Contents

A DANGEROUS ENCOUNTER

PART ONE

A Sunday Morning in Paris

1

It was the first Sunday in September, a blue day. Around this time the splendor of summer often gathers for a final flourish before autumn colors begin to glow. The nights are cooler; this makes the dawn moist and the morning mild and pleasant. The foliage of the trees has a deeper hue, standing out as if embossed against the sky. In the cities, too, it has grown cooler; there is a hint of luxury and gaiety in the air.

Gerhard was standing in front of the small square of the Trinité. The gardeners had already planted the beds with the first autumn flowers. On a narrow border, shooting up out of bright green, the Indian Canna was still in bloom. The row was interspersed with circular beds from which, many-starred, a blue aster rose up. The petals were radiant in the sunshine. Bees and flower flies were buzzing around them. An admiral with brick-red stripes was resting on their soft crown. It turned slowly on the velvet cushion, opening its wings at leisurely intervals. It must have come from far away, flying in over the high roofs. A second one joined it. The butterflies began circling each other and, floating upwards, disappeared into the sky.

From Saint-Lazare came the bright sound of boys' voices; they were calling out the Sunday papers. The bells began to ring, and a crowd in festive attire emerged from the church doors and walked toward the carriages that were waiting on the square. It was a wedding procession. Grains of rice were strewn on the carpet in front of the young couple. This spectacle interrupted the dreamy contemplation in which Gerhard was absorbed. He mingled with the passers-by, who flocked together and dispersed again as the carriages moved away. Then, like someone who does not care what direction he takes, he turned into the Rue Blanche and sauntered up the hill.

It was cooler in the shadow of the houses; the streets had just been sprayed. The water ran down along the curbs. The quarter, otherwise full of noise and bustle, was quieter this morning. Missing were the vendors who sold fish, fruit, and vegetables in the streets. There were only flower stands today. The city seemed emptier and hence rather solemn; a large part of the population was spending the day on the banks of the river or in the suburbs. One could still see the last coaches heading out; they were crammed to the hood with young men and their flamboyantly dressed companions. They would be out in the country by midday and return late. Here the horses went at a walking pace; their hooves slid on the steep pavement.

Although Gerhard had been living in the city for over a year, each of these walks held mysteries for him. He hardly had the feeling that he was crossing squares and streets; rather, it seemed as if he were striding through the rooms and corridors of a large unknown house or wandering through shafts that had been driven into layers of rock. In certain lanes, at certain crossings, the enchantment was especially powerful. Gerhard hardly gave the matter a thought. It was less the monuments and palaces that impressed him as witnesses of an historic past, but rather the anonymous life that this great city had formed like a coral reef—the substance of its destiny. Hence he felt particularly at home in those quarters that had grown up contrary to all rules of architecture, pieced together haphazardly over the course of centuries. Countless unknowns had lived here, suffered and been happy. Countless others still inhabited this ground. The very mortar was imbued with their life. The energy was extremely concentrated, indeed miraculous. And he was always inspired by the feeling that this miracle could take shape any moment: with a letter, a message, an encounter, or an adventure, as in grottos and enchanted gardens.

On these walks he was filled with great tenderness. He was tuned like a string at rest which scarcely needs the hand that plays upon it. A breath, a ray of sunshine would suffice to make it vibrate. There was an aura of innocence about him, apparent even to dull eyes.

Gerhard turned into the Rue Chaptal. The street was deserted. On the left, placards glared from both walls of a blind alley. It led to a tiny theater which, together with the dance halls and other places of entertainment, gave the hill its stamp. The quarter seemed devoid of life, but it would light up magically as soon as night fell.

Gerhard had heard of this theater—it numbered among

the bizarre places that foreigners make sure to visit. One had to see it, like the Catacombs, the Morgue on the Ile de la Cité, or the large Cemetery of Père-Lachaise. Like these, it was a dismal place; only macabre pieces were performed. These copied the style of the old Punch and Judy and employed the same lurid motifs with the rigidness of marionettes. Generally, the visitors were not inclined to return, but a clientele had formed around this locale that matched its peculiar character. It was recruited from the local underworld: men with powerful chins and shaved necks, accompanied by girls in gaudy makeup. One saw eccentrics as well: broken-down old men and foreigners bearing the scars of a puritanical upbringing, also adolescents full of voracious curiosity. The bow was quivering; it had not yet been put to the test. Or it was worn out, either by power and wealth or by profligacy; it could only be made taut by the most powerful stimuli. When the director's three thumps had resounded, they came together under the spell of naked cruelty. Then there was the implicit blasphemy that the theater had been installed in the chapel of an abandoned monastery, and the nature of the place had scarcely changed. It was as though one were sitting in the choir stalls during a Black Mass celebrated by evil monks.

Gerhard stopped in front of the entrance and studied the play-bills:

THE NEW BLUEBEARD
REALISTIC PLAY IN THREE ACTS
BY LÉON GRANDIER

Then came the cast of characters and the actors' names. The letters appeared to have been drawn with a brush; they were spattered with drops of red. Above them was a picture of a bearded man with a knife between his teeth, leaping out of a house window.

The subject was current. The papers were full of reports about the atrocities of a murderer who had been stalking the streets of London for months. It seemed that he chose only women as his victims and that he had a marked preference for prostitutes, small-time actresses, singers in dives, demimonde in general. The whole thing was repugnant, as if some predatory fish had found its way into the sewers, and with each murder the agitation grew; it spread to all the cities of Europe. This monster seemed to combine extreme audacity with the wariness of an animal—no one had caught a glimpse of him yet.

Just as there is nothing tasteless and nothing horrible that does not attract people, so it was here, too. In all big cities there are spirits who are lured by the call of the underworld. It was no wonder, then, that this theater, where no play was performed that did not show bloodshed, seized on the sensational. Gerhard hurried past; it was no place for him.

2

It was only a few steps to the Rue Pigalle. Gerhard followed it up to the square bearing the same name. The wide boulevard that cuts across it was busier; two rows of carriages were rolling smoothly along on it, moving now at a walk, now at a trot, when the drivers stroked the horses' flanks with their whips. In the back, men with high hats lounged, dreaming of their approaching midday meal, married couples, too, and ladies shading their faces with parasols.

The tables in front of the cafés were crowded. Waiters in white jackets were scurrying out the doors; they were carrying glasses filled with different-colored drinks and placing large carafes of ice water beside them. The customers were absorbed in conversations or in reading the newspapers, when they were not casually watching the flow of carriages and pedestrians that passed close by their chairs. Occasionally they nodded to acquaintances.

The middle section of the large artery formed an avenue. It was set off by a double row of trees. In the evening, innumerable colored lamps turned the strip into a promenade for great throngs of people. At this hour, riders could be seen trotting along in its green shade. In some places idlers stood around in groups watching sword swallowers and acrobats who had rolled out carpets and were performing their tricks. Then they would go around with a tin funnel and collect copper coins. After a short break, they sounded a horn to announce their next number.

Gerhard was walking on the side of the street where the Collège Rollin rises to view. Here the sidewalk was less crowded; an occasional stroller walked by. Just as in all big cities there are climates that make two sides of the same street different, the women here seemed more elegantly dressed than in the cafés across the way. They floated slowly past in their Sunday attire, the delicate veils scarcely concealing their features. Despite the heat they were wearing long gloves. They held their parasols open, taking great care that not one ray of sunlight fell upon faces whose large eyes sparkled. Now and then they caught sight of Gerhard with a look of surprise and then lowered their gaze dreamily to the ground.

Gerhard heard the rustle of silk, when their skirts nearly brushed against him, like the murmur of a distant tide carried on the breeze. And he was always seized with awe as before a sublime painting, as if goddesses were offering themselves to his gaze; fairies and enchantresses followed at their heels.

He was always surprised, indeed amazed when he saw them in the company of men. To approach them struck him as impudent; the very thought of it was inconceivable. But wonderful, uplifting conversations would be possible with them; he felt this intuitively. Yet he would be incapable of opening his mouth—this he knew for sure. In his dreams, he was their servant, their confidant as well. He saw himself as their deliverer from perils and his destiny bound up with theirs amidst vicissitudes that are depicted in novels.

Surely nothing in his appearance could account for this timidity. Almost all young people go through such a phase of susceptibility. Perhaps in Gerhard's case it was excessive; it also lasted longer than usual. This may have been because his mother had died young; he had scarcely known her. In his memory her image had been transfigured; he thought back on her with veneration. Entrusted with the affairs of a petty sovereign, his father was often away on trips and had his son brought up in boarding schools. Then he had sent him away to study in Göttingen. Gerhard lived there with an aunt, who with age had grown a bit peculiar. Life in her big house, which hardly anyone ever visited, suited his penchant for solitude, which he enjoyed. The world of books and dreams sufficed to give him a higher sense of well-being, although he was not always able to avoid the claims made upon him by society—by his professors, his fellow students, and his compeers. He had completed his studies in the prescribed time; then a distant relative, whom he called uncle, Herr von Zimmern, had brought him to Paris and gotten him attached to the embassy with one of those titles that look good on calling cards.

Gerhard's idiosyncrasies, which aroused sympathy as well as consternation, were also conspicuous in his new sur- roundings. They gradually became more obvious. Recently after a reception, before they retired, Frau von Zimmern had sat up for a while with her husband in the drawing room and discussed the guests.

"Your nephew is charming—but don't you have the impression that he's lacking something? I find him terribly childlike for someone going on twenty-five. You should look after him a bit more. He's too much of a dreamer."

The ambassador, who was tired after a long day, smiled. He caressed her arm:

"We would do better to look after him less. I knew what I was doing when I suggested he take his own apartment. You regard one of his assets as a flaw, Elisabeth. Gerhard is extremely well-bred, respectful, chivalrous. Look at his face; it doesn't lie. I'm fond of the boy and am always pleased when I see him in the midst of all these smug people and their vain perfection. Of course, they know the price of things and their purpose. In my youth, dreamers like him were more common; later on they played a role, often prominent, in world affairs. It's not a good sign that ever since the founding of the new Empire they are dying out."

Herr von Zimmern rose from his armchair and, bending over the lamp, lit a last cigar.

"He takes after his father; we were friends during my Oldenburg years. He then became the shrewd homme d'affaires that you know. I predict something similar for Gerhard. There are encounters that crystallize what is at first only vague rumination."

Frau von Zimmern had stood up too; it was already late. She closed the conversation:

"I'm sure you're right. Of course, there are also evil encounters. It's not so much Gerhard's naiveté that bothers me, although it often oversteps the bounds. He makes up for it with his manner. Everyone likes him; that offsets what is ridiculous. Sometimes he reminds me of a doll, a creature conceived in a strange realm, that was cast by mistake into a world whose rules and pitfalls it doesn't know. Therein lies the danger. To exist, such a creature would need the aid of partners who, like him, come from far-off places—children, fairies, wise magicians."

The ambassador took leave of her with a hand kiss:

"I know that at least *one* benevolent spirit is watching out for him. He will be grateful to you."

3

Gerhard was of medium height and delicate, almost boyish build. The easy gait, the soft hair, the thin face scarcely touched by the sun gave the impression of a person who is at once strong and in need of protection: who has power without the means of realizing it. Indeed, some treasures cannot be turned into gain. Combined with this was a sense of contradiction—like "inhibited performer." In a calculating, well-defined world, this charm was out of place; in paintings, even those of contemporaries, it would have been less surprising.

Two girls carrying portfolios under their arms walked past him; they were no doubt coming back from their music lesson. One nudged the other and said: "Aren't you ashamed of yourself, turning around to look at men on the street?"

Her friend laughed: "But that's not a man—it's a Prince Charming."

Gerhard did not understand the nature of the glances that were directed at him. They settled on him with an expression of surprise and then dreamily turned away. Once they had passed, some of the women touched their belts or quickly ran a hand over their hair. He found these glances strange and enigmatic; he felt threatened by them.

The shady side of the boulevard had been pleasant; Gerhard had now reached the Place d'Anvers: a narrow rectangle planted with trees. It was just about time for lunch. On the corner of the Rue de Gérando was a restaurant: "At the Dukes of Burgundy." Its sign was a flat bowl like those wine-tasters at well-known vineyards wear like a medal around their necks.

A table covered with a white cloth was set up in front of the door. Spread out on the linen, still steaming as they came out of the pot, were fruits de mer.

Bright red lobsters beckoned with extended claws, beside them an array of rust-colored crawfish already halved by the knife. They were surrounded by garlands of shrimps and prawns. The pink-ribbed shells of the large scallops were gaping, revealing their white flesh. Standing at the foot of the table were low baskets with the first oysters; they were wrapped in wet sea moss. It was as if the net's catch had spilled out of a horn of plenty. The display showed that the kitchen was optimally prepared for Sunday guests. The first could be seen entering through the glass door.

An elderly gentleman slowly walked past, giving Gerhard a fleeting glance. As he moved on he seemed to reflect, then he came back and politely lifted his hat: "Ah—Herr zum Busche—what brings you to my neighborhood at this hour?"

Gerhard recalled the dark eyes with their thin, arching brows now examining him with cool curiosity. They peered alertly out of a pale, sickly face. Their owner was perhaps a little over sixty; his name was Ducasse. Although he belonged to an old family, he was only to be seen on the fringes of society: at the races, at the gaming tables, and at luncheons. Above all, he could be found in the entourage of rich strangers who regularly visited the city; he was considered a connoisseur of choice diversions. In this respect, he would have been more at home in the previous century, as the friend of princes who reveled before the deluge. Now he was dependent on their grandchildren in a time of lost illusions, in which pleasures too had coarsened. This kept the mild disgust alive and with it the mark of suffering, for the cook must always know more than his guests.

There had been a breach in this existence, after which the trappings of great wealth had dwindled away, and what followed was not apt to improve his reputation. His prominent benefactors did more to keep him in vogue than in good standing. One might meet Monsieur Ducasse in the embassy, but never at the salons where Gerhard's aunt received her guests. It is not unlikely that this circumstance played a role in what follows. Monsieur Ducasse was still sensitive on this point; nevertheless, he seemed to be delighted by this chance encounter. As if to ingratiate himself, he touched Gerhard's arm and said:

"You did well to stay in the city. Even on Sunday one needn't be bored here. That's a prejudice."

Then, pointing with the pommel of his cane toward the display table:

"A still life—wouldn't you say? The house is good, the wine cellar is famous."

He qualified his judgment:

"At least as far as the Burgundy is concerned. I see you're deliberating, as if you were going to have lunch. You should go to Voisin. There you'll find the best the sea has to offer. It would be a pleasure for me to invite you there. . . ."

He hesitated a moment:

"Unless you prefer to be alone."

It had actually been Gerhard's intention to spend this Sunday by himself and far away from the center of the city where one always ran into acquaintances. But the invitation had touched the childlike quality in him that was his distinguishing trait. Older people were invariably the grown-ups for him; their realm was quite separate from his own. The way they moved, thought, acted was incomprehensible and presupposed mysteries. They replaced the uncertain with assurance. Gerhard always felt pleased when one of them took an interest in him. That is why he quickly accepted the invitation, while adding apologetically:

". . . although I'm afraid my company will bore you."

"You needn't worry about that," Ducasse reassured him and signaled a coachman who was slowly driving past.

The carriage was ramshackle and tossed up and down on its springs. A toilworn white nag drew it ploddingly down the hill; the horse probably had known service in the Second Empire. The sun was beating down, making Ducasse's face blink and twitch. It was a sickly, ravaged face in whose eyes, nevertheless, the will still flashed unbroken. This gave it something compelling, lent it a kind of magnetism.

Gerhard, who lived in a dreamworld, was not familiar with the anecdotes attached to this man's name. Thus he could not know that this situation—that of a dandy who does not let the shabbiness of the vehicle he is sitting in affect his sense of superiority—was typical of Léon Ducasse. It symbolized the fate he had to bear, had to master as Brummell had his in Calais. The sarcasm of the capital had tested its cutting edge on it, only to accomodate it later, once it had come into fashion. This demanded a certain steadfastness.

A dozen years had already passed since the famous "Return from Longchamps." That was the title of the caricature that had amused all Paris the day after his ruin. It showed Léon enthroned in an open fiacre amidst the tumult of luxurious horses and carriages as they returned from the racetrack. With his chin resting casually on his cane, the white chrysanthemum in his buttonhole, he exposed himself to the stares with his usual nonchalance. Just as misfortune reveals a person's true mettle, that episode had proved that Ducasse's significance was not based on vast wealth, on the millions he had squandered on building projects, festivities, and works of art. This had come to him by way of a fabulous marriage, only to disappear like a mirage along with his wife. What remained as the last flowering of an old family was his infallible taste, the knowledge of the exquisite things of this world. This knowledge, in fact, has no need of resources, since its strength resides in sound judgment. A smile can annihilate pretentions or confirm them. In this respect, Ducasse was as much admired as he was feared.

4

If the catastrophe had left a wound in Ducasse, then it was the hatred for everything feminine, which may always have been dormant in him, but now became overt. The love of women had never meant much to him, but there are forms of refinement which seem to imitate it, indeed surpass it, as certain artificial flowers do natural ones. One thing he was expert at: giving beauty, like a pearl, the setting it deserves. Yet the moment it attained perfection, he would lapse into boredom and irony. That had been his downfall.

On the other hand, material restraints had only served to confirm and strengthen him in his real inclinations. The power over beautiful things does not, of course, lie in the fact of ownership. Rather, Ducasse was indispensible to owners because he could attest to the true value of their possessions. He offered proof of their authenticity. It is correct to regard doubt as a sign that an epoch is nearing its end, as a symptom of decline. As long as it is directed against the highest values, life is still tolerable, indeed sensual pleasures are even enhanced, but then doubt encroaches on the visible treasures as well, those in which the senses delight. It is like mildew that spreads from the ceiling to the wallpaper, causing its patterns to fade. As suspicion increases, so do disgust and falsification. Finally even the simplest things become suspect: the glass of water, the food on the table, the spoon that carries it to the mouth.

In such times, men like Ducasse are true helpers in need for the powerful and wealthy. They banish tedium and restore good conscience. Property gives rise to fear when we lose the power to control it. The very sight of food piled up on the table is oppressive to one who is sated. He must then become a disdainer, a miser, or a spendthrift—unless one can awaken new illusions in him. Ducasse had made this his duty. If money and influence were like instruments, then he could show how they were played and what melodies were possible. Essentially, he was always the giver and passed on what he had inherited.

That explains why the wreck did not impinge on his way of life. It struck the ship, but not the helmsman. His old friends stuck by him—even profited more from him, now that his own affairs occupied him less.

From then on his mode of living grew simple, even Spartan, in everything except his appearance. He lived in a small apartment with a servant who had remained loyal to him since his youth. He had settled there with some old furniture and unmatched pieces—flotsam that survived his shipwreck. Occasionally a visitor would express a particular liking for a painting or a carpet. Then Ducasse would hint that this desire could be satisfied—which did not turn out to his disadvantage. He then filled the gap at the dealers, who still held him in high regard.

In this way, the unlimited means which had been at his disposal continued to yield interest. Extravagance had led to his proficiency in all matters of taste. Only value counted; the price was unimportant.

He had once dreamt of restoring about himself the old society with its forms, its colors, its gaiety. He had had to learn that this sort of thing at best leads to the successful illusions of historical masquerades. Still, he possessed a kind of hereditary honesty which obliged him to use authentic decorations. He often said that he did not regret having paid dearly for his experience. This benefited his friends, who were less worried about costs than they were about authenticity. A horse, a painting, a piece of jewelry, a country house—in short, whatever Ducasse had approved stood every test. The same held true for the festivities over which he presided as maître de plaisir. The host and his guests knew then that they had amused themselves. It was even said of Ducasse that he arranged marriages.

Over the years, this role turned out to be untenable. The part of go-between eroded it. The ideal go-between is one who appreciates the value of things without wanting them for himself. He escorts the bride to her groom in her wedding dress and is satisfied when he has closed the bedroom door behind them. Yet: if he lacks kindness, hatred will mount up inside him—hatred for the pleasures and for those enjoying them.

The path this man had taken showed that one cannot cling to refinement. It took him from the role of patron to that of cultivated mentor, but then to eccentricity, boredom, and finally cynicism. It could not escape such keen eyes as these that beauty was depleted at the same rate that society destroyed itself. Although Ducasse profited from decay, he despised the circumstances in which he was forced to live: those of the impoverished squire who conducts wealthy strangers through sites of faded revelries—indeed, who occasionally reproduces them theatrically. On these occasions there was no lack of crude jokes and improprieties, but it was prudent to overlook them. Essentially, he led the life of a dandy who played the buffoon for the demos and sought to take revenge for it on everything that was still intact.

5

"Now, dear friend—what do you say to that—doesn't the sea work wonders?"

Ducasse was pointing to the dishes that the waiter had just placed on the table. Shimmering on a bed of crushed ice were six oysters, which Gerhard found exquisite. They rested like pale moons in their mother-of-pearl shells; they emanated the fragrance of seaweed. A ray of sunshine fell through the curtain, refracting on the fine crystals; its reflections undulated on the carafe of golden wine. The chairs were covered with a red material; that gave the room a warm, intimate atmosphere. Gerhard was easily susceptible to this; he had a sense of well-being in this place. He replied:

"The oysters are really superb; but they would taste twice as good if you would join me."

At these words a shadow passed over Ducasse's face. For some time now only the simplest dishes agreed with him, without any salt or fat; painful crises were sure to follow the slightest transgression. A little silver bowl of noodles stood on the table before him; the waiter poured him a glass of Vichy water. One could see that eating bored him, indeed irritated him. Nevertheless, he took pains to conceal this, and with delicate, almost loving meticulousness selected the wines and dishes for his companion. At the same time he tested the sharpness of his wit on the guests, who were nearly all familiar to him. From a sideboard standing in front of the lift, their own and three other tables were being served with silent attentiveness. At one table sat an elderly couple: a lady in a black velvet dress, whose décolletage was adorned by a string of pearls, and her companion, who despite the heat was wearing a gray frock coat buttoned up to the neck. The two of them ate, scarcely exchanging a word, now and then raising a glass to their lips.

"The lady looks tired," said Gerhard, who was sitting across from them.

Ducasse turned his head and twisted his face into a pained smile:

"Of course—being ugly is trying. Besides, her husband fled from his creditors to Turkey—they say he's been hiding out there for two years."

He nodded, then, as if wanting to temper his judgment, added:

"Incidentally, he's considered the most decent one in the family. As for the couple, nobody knows whether he keeps her or she him. A writer whose works you can find among the trash along the quays. Recently he published a collection of photographs—without a doubt the best book he has written."

Listening to Ducasse, one was sure to get a calamitous picture of society, in which meanness, ugliness, even crime were smouldering beneath the varnish. A long study of human weaknesses and shortcomings must have gone before. Ducasse's disgust took satisfaction in this. "Ardent delight" was the word for it.

Schooled in a politeness that required pretending one did not know what one knew about each other, Ducasse did not think it necessary to restrain himself in front of Gerhard. Like almost everyone who met the young German, he looked upon him as someone with an almost appalling lack of sophistication: as one of those eccentrics that are often found in old families. His manner provoked a response: whereas some could not help but like him, others were keen to find out how far they could go with such a person before he caught on.

Indeed, Gerhard seemed not to notice the fishhooks that Ducasse was putting out for his vulgar curiosity. At the points where he expected a smile he saw himself disappointed. His companion's face showed always the same untroubled cheerfulness. Ducasse shrugged his shoulders and had the sommelier bring champagne; after diluting it, he charily drank to Gerhard's health—he also had to be careful about his heart. Then he broached a different subject:

"When I see you here at the table, Herr zum Busche," he began in a half condescending, half confidential tone, "I am truly surprised that on a beautiful day like this you're without company. You're right not to have gone to the country—particularly since you're not a hunter like your uncle. But you're wrong not to be spending the afternoon with a beautiful woman."

Gerhard blushed at being spoken to so directly, although the subject was of burning interest to him. He gave as a reply:

"All the same, it does take two, Monsieur Ducasse."

Ducasse was startled; was he to take that as a joke or not? Then he grew animated:

"That coming from a young man like you, who should have no problem other than choosing? Haven't you noticed that wherever you turn up women make eyes as though the sacrament were being carried past? I'd take Paris by storm with your youth and your charm. Just look over there at the way the Countess Kargané has been eyeing you ever since you came in."

6

In saying this, Ducasse had motioned with his head toward a lady sitting at one of the small tables in the company of an old man. Gerhard had noticed her at first glance: a woman who was bound to attract attention everywhere and also excite admiration—she was beautiful.

The tall, slender figure was dressed in a black outfit, which made it stand out from the red divan. She was resting her head casually against her hand and seemed to be listening to her companion, while every now and then she would observe the other guests. Her face was striking in its regularity, whose effect at a distance was like that of a mask or an actress who has skillfully simplified her features. Her dark brown hair was thick and supple like the fur of an animal that is pleasant to stroke. It covered her ears and half her forehead. The nose was a bit too short, giving her face, especially when she raised her eyes, a touch of impertinence. But the eyes were large and shining like gray agates set in marble; the blue shadows surrounding them made them seem even bigger. A simple elegance endowed her with a self-containedness, a strict proportion like a jewel sufficient in its own luster. In contrast to this was a distracted dreaminess.

Beauty and agitation were at variance in this face. Misfortune always ensues when power is inherited without the self-assurance needed to control it. Just as a large fortune only causes mischief when it passes to a spendthrift, beauty can prove to be a dangerous endowment for whoever inherits it, as well as for others.

Ducasse, who was familiar with the fringes of society, had an eye for the precarious. He knew that it was best to avoid the Countess. The trouble was not that she had the traits of a large cat. Even tigresses have their own law. Here it was the presence of disorder that made one wary, a lack of equilibrium. Cause and effect were faultily connected. What went on inside this head was unpredictable. It might have looked something like a railway station where pure whim opens and shuts the barriers, throws switches. Anyone present was exposed to the danger of senseless collisions. Beauty was a glittering lure in which a hook was concealed.

In the Middle Ages one might have suspected such a woman of being a sorceress; in the eighteenth century, she might have passed for one of those grandes dames who did as they pleased. Now one could sense an exasperated weakness there. The erosion of existing forms was far advanced, although outwardly they seemed intact. Names still carried their weight, wealth was still inherited as in the old days. Yet these cases had become equivocal, in so far as some still bore the stamp of tradition, others already of decline—and the latter with more compelling inevitability. The old families were still flourishing, but the fruit had become barren and hybrid.

7

"It's her father," said Ducasse, indicating the old man, "Admiral Jeannot."

Gerhard knew the name; it was closely associated with colonial history. One usually saw the admiral with his daughter when there was strife in her marriage; it then fell to him to appease her. This was difficult, which is why he preferred to take her to restaurants where the conversation was kept within bounds. Then there were the fruitless discussions with his son-in-law.

Actually things had not gone well between Irene and Kargané from the very beginning, since he indulged his inclinations as ruthlessly as a freebooter and did what he pleased. Irene's mother had died young; her daughter had grown up almost like an amazon, while her father was nearly always away at sea. Kargané had served in the navy as well. Jeannot had already known him and thought highly of him before the two were married.

Kargané had retired as captain; from the start he had been a difficult subordinate, but brilliant on board his own ship. Intelligent, punctilious, brave, a good comrade and pleasant company—certainly brutal as well, but this was more an advantage in his profession. Such a character is suited for the highest positions, provided he does not undermine himself. He will only realize his talents fully at the top—but where could one still find such positions in the Republic? It was men like him who within a few decades had founded a colonial empire—opposed not only by the world, but by many at home as well.

"You can't say I didn't warn you. You wanted it." Irene did not like hearing this, but in fact the admiral had had misgivings from the very beginning. Beauty alone was not enough to bind a man like Kargané, and what would happen when he found out what lay hidden beneath it?

Otherwise it was a splendid match, in terms both of name and fortune. Since they were quite taken with each other, Jeannot would not persist in his objections. And wouldn't Irene have simply ignored him? One could only hope that the union would be a happy one; the prospects were not unfavorable.

Yet from the very first day it was apparent that in this marriage two characters had come together who were too strong for each other. Following his resignation Kargané had remained true to his habits—oscillating between activity and idleness as was the way with seamen. He loved changes of location and scenery, journeys to the edges of the known world, adventures in foreign ports where he lived under an assumed name, debauchery coarse and refined. Rumor placed him in Aden in the uniform of a common sailor and in the Sultan's palace in Cairo; on these excursions, he benefited from a physique of iron and superb orientation. That gave him, even when he was drunk or under the influence of drugs, a residue of consciousness: he knew his limits, whatever the circumstances. And given his means, these limits were far-flung. One might speak of a technical morality, as proclaimed by 19th-century moralists: the doctrine that morals change with latitude had become the voyager's practice.

Kargané's absences began to last longer after a distant relative had left him estates in Transylvania. Little was known about this; it seems that out there, amidst great expanses of forest, he had fitted out a castle on the model of the Duc de Blangis—but these were only rumors, albeit of a dark nature.

Yet the fact was that the life he led in Paris had grown more stable. He lived here quietly like a champion who uses up his surplus energy on distant courts. He was seen at parties and receptions, at gatherings of former naval officers, in the fencing hall, gambling at the Jockey Club. He was good company, high-spirited, generous, an amusing conversationalist; he was always surrounded by friends.

One of his portraits was considered especially well done; it showed him in a blue jacket, his hands stuck in his side pockets, in front of a pale blue sky such as occasionally brightens the Brittany coast at the beginning of autumn. The painter who had done this picture loved blue tones; he had given the dark beard framing the tanned face a shade more than was true to life. In the background were hints of masts and sails, sifted and dispersed by the light, as was now becoming the fashion.

It seemed that Kargané had developed political ambitions. Perhaps he was bored in Paris. He avoided associations and actions that are damaging in elections. There were rumors about him, but nothing tangible. In the foreground stood the cheerful seaman, who had his weaknesses, but lived and let live. Moreover, people were not squeamish these days. He had begun with a moderate criticism of the naval build-up, which he presented in various articles and lectures. That was a good point of departure.

When he returned from his voyages, there would be domestic crises like storms brought about by the accumulation of great tensions. He had soon realized that Irene would not be fobbed off with the role he intended for her, that of a plaything removed from its box only when the need arises. She was too strong, too unpredictable for that. Her upbringing had accustomed her to great freedom of movement. His will, despotic beneath a polished surface, had not been able to break her. Like so many men, he had married the type that was least suited to him. Even the attempt to establish a common ground on which they could appear together had failed: he was unable to run a house with her in which guests could be entertained. From the very beginning the atmosphere was either icy or too tense. They could count themselves lucky if an evening went off without a scandal. Kargané even had the impression that there were guests who came expecting one.

At bottom, she had remained more dependent on him than he was on her. This dependency had turned into hostility, even hatred. Kargané treated her at first like an animal tamer who wants to inspire fear. But Irene was fearless and did not shrink from quarrels either privately or in front of others; it even seemed as if she were bent on them. At times Kargané asked himself whether the agitation that impelled her was not a symptom of a mental illness. Once they would have locked her up, but there was no chance of that anymore.

Finally he had decided to allow her some freedom; for him that was still the lesser evil. Perhaps it would relieve him most if she took a lover; he had even suggested it once following one of those scenes that had left him exhausted. "But I wouldn't like to hear about it from the footman," he had added.

Meanwhile, more had happened along these lines than would have suited him. The city had a thousand eyes and ears, and society lived on gossip. There was not one of Irene's rendezvous that the Captain did not hear about in all its details. Apparently, without success, she was on the lookout for a gigolo. "If she had at least taken somebody from the navy, but when it comes to men she has no instinct."

The Captain also had her watched when he was away on trips. This was seen to by Mauclerc, his close friend, who had formerly served under him in the navy. Kargané was bored by business matters, and Mauclerc had acted as his agent; among other things he managed the Count's hunting ground near Rambouillet. The Count had hunting friends in France as well as in Transylvania; some shared in his political ambitions, others in his pleasures.

Only the day before Mauclerc had reported to him again, and the chief had said, "Damn it, the woman is pushing me too far." It came at just the wrong moment.

8

Ducasse, who was sipping his watered-down champagne while observing the clientele, easily guessed that there was trouble again at the Karganés. The Countess was talking excitedly to her father, who now and again laid a comforting hand on her arm. The Captain had recently returned; he had already been seen here and there. Ducasse regarded him as an adventurer with big plans who perhaps wanted to become a Minister—anything was possible in an era in which the likes of Gallifet appeared on the platform. It was curious that such offices were coveted—after all, they brought only trouble and unsavory company. Kargané seemed intent on proving that he was no cleverer than the others. Better things might have been expected from him, considering what one had heard.

Ducasse began to feel the drab dish, although only half finished, stirring inside him. He ordered a glass of water and poured a white powder into it. When he had swallowed the chalky mixture with a grimace, he looked dreadfully wasted. It was a calamity: although his diet had become increasingly simple, his stomach was less and less able to cope. He had to treat it like a retort, whose processes he kept going with pills and drops. The moment he ate anything, he could feel his stomach surging and boiling like a cauldron. He had only vague notions as to what was wrong, and sought the advice of doctors who were fashionable, but after every meal there was a kind of agony—a dread that could scarcely be controlled. These spasms were like the attacks of a wild animal that overtook him again and again, despite every precaution. Lately other organs seemed to be affected—in his right side he felt a burning, a heaviness that evoked the unpleasant image of a flatiron. Then there were the horrors of insomnia. They were the worst, because they forced him to agonize relentlessly over his illness, while time crept by like a red snail.

He had had no idea that fear could gain such a strangle-hold. His heart began to pound in ever more rapid, ever more violent drumrolls; he had to struggle for breath. His thoughts reared like a horse shying at the abyss. Right at his feet was the void. He was staring into it—it was darker and more horrible than anything one could imagine, and terribly still. He was tempted to scream and would have wept if he had been able. He felt the cold sweat on his forehead, the bitter taste in his mouth. Then it subsided, the crisis had passed; he went into the bathroom, washed and rubbed himself down.

These attacks came over him during the brief span in which even Montmartre was silent. His hands still trembled when he lit the nightlamp. A faint glow fell upon the furniture in the room, which recalled an atelier. Ducasse would begin to calm down; he paced back and forth over the rugs as if in a tent. Then he heard the carriages as they rolled toward Les Halles; the stars still shone through the skylight.

Once he had loved this hour. Now it brought back memories of magnificent days and their abundance. He knew that he had reached the point where pleasures became cerebral, immaterial. Their refinement and their harmony had been the aim of the festivities that he had created and on which he squandered his fortune. The question remained, whose enjoyment was greater: that of the host or his guests, the director or the spectators, the inspired conductor or his listeners. Ducasse was carried away by the sight of his own ingenuity.

Once again he immersed himself in his days of glory: the nocturnal party beside the lake in the woods, the famous masked ball in his townhouse. There had been hours where the enchantment was perfect, hours which nobody would forget. Life was the art of arts, because it made all the others subservient—not only the artists, but also the craftsmen, from the architects and jewelers, down to the chefs and coachmen. He, Ducasse, had known how to awaken in his workmen and servants the invaluable ambition that elevated their zeal into art. There were still craftsmen who worked in the old traditions and servants to whom service meant more than a mere job. He had succeeded in uniting people again in a Living Picture, a great symphony. Perhaps it was nostalgia that had made him do it, the insatiable longing for a vanished age. Of course, he was bailing with a sieve. All the same, it had been worth the effort: to transform the tomb into a luminous grotto—as a protest against a world in which bleak ugliness prevailed on all levels. His had been Pyrrhic victories like those Ludwig of Bavaria had achieved with his castles. But Ducasse had no regrets.

Some said that he squandered thirty million, others thought this estimate was too low. He had ennobled this money, which had been amassed in Chicago, had made it serve a higher purpose. In the happy days of their marriage, Daisy had appreciated this; she had been proud of him and of the fabulous shimmer he spread about her. And she had forgiven him much. In time, he had grown too negligent toward her. Women like her want to be worshiped. A malicious quip had precipitated the end. Visitors being shown about the house had been allowed a look at Daisy's bedroom. "And here is the chapel of penance"—this remark, which was passed on to her immediately, had hurt her more deeply than his infidelity. He had never been able to refrain from such bons mots; malice was his birth defect.

Now he was compelled by fate to be bored at the banquets of the rich, for whom he played the maître des plaisirs. He sat at tables where master chefs like Ali Bab and Escoffier displayed their skills. But he had to let dish after dish go by untouched while he watched the others feasting. That was his lot.

9

Ducasse, who observed all the more keenly the more he suffered, had not been exaggerating; it was striking, during the pauses in the conversation with her father, with what intentness the Countess fixed her eyes on Gerhard. She was scrutinizing him like a huntress. Perhaps she remembered having seen the young man and was trying to place him, but it was also possible that an interest of the sort Ducasse presumed was involved.

Almost tiring of his guest, Ducasse indulged in a series of combinations while continuing the conversation. If he could pair off this young fool and this half-crazy woman, who were obviously taken with each other, then it would inevitably result in a scandal. Ducasse began to feel a little better now at the thought of Frau von Zimmern; it gave him the pleasure an artist feels when he sketches a composition. Quite aside from the grudge he bore the ambassadress, he was fascinated by the motif as such, like a pyrotechnist who develops in his little room a set of rockets with which he plans to astonish, but also terrify a sophisticated public.

He reflected. Should he simply write the Countess a letter? As far as she was concerned there was no risk involved. She was known to be eccentric. Everyone who came near her could tell that she was not squeamish and that excesses were more apt to amuse her. For all her grandiosity, there was clearly something equivocal about her, and then there was the likelihood of sudden outbursts. Such figures move like the knight in a game of chess. With the decline of society they had grown more common and more unabashed; they ran off with band leaders or ruined themselves in some other way in the shortest time. Many years later, after they had closed their eyes in some attic or hospital, their names would appear once again in the newspapers. In the old days they would have been stuck in a convent.

On the red sofa she resembled a painting by his friend Lautrec—one of his more elegant models beside a rich lover. Certainly boldness could not offend her. On the other hand, Kargané was not to be trifled with. That was the point, but Ducasse himself could not get involved. He might get his fingers burned if he wasn't careful.

Ducasse felt a glimmer of health and vitality return to him. With renewed benevolence he turned to Gerhard and had the waiter fill his glass. He repeated:

"I'd take Paris by storm if I were your age and had your looks."

Ducasse was recalling his own youth. He had been able to choose and had chosen the wealthiest. Her fortune had overshadowed all others, but it only acquired significance under the sway of illusion. Ducasse had put the money to its proper use, and Daisy had understood immediately that he was its true, its legitimate custodian. In those days people were fascinated not only by his background and breeding, but by his exceptional charm. Like Gerhard he had been of delicate build, but of startling presence. Up to then, Daisy had only known how much things cost; he taught her a new science, opened up a more beautiful world. Through him she discovered her true significance, her real worth.

Ducasse breathed a soul into her. She became his creature, in her carriage and posture as well as in the jewels and clothes she wore. She spoke, felt, and thought as he did. An excellent pedagogue, he had first given her an awareness of her aesthetic value, implanted it in her mind, and then set about cultivating its outward appearance. It had been a love founded on good taste, and hence more substantial than any passion. By catering to people's vanity, particularly that of women, one couldn't go wrong. The woman on the red divan would be as accessible as any other. Again he laid his emaciated hand on Gerhard's arm:

"You see, my dear friend, you're too timid, you often blush for no reason and you live in a dreamworld. You should discard that habit. You must wake up and come to grips with the world—then your dreams will become reality."

10

Ducasse touched upon a subject there which had often preoccupied Gerhard, though from the opposite point of view. Feelings were what inspired him rather than thoughts, but he did not let them show on the surface. Many people, particularly the young, waste themselves on novels they do not dare to write, let alone act out. Gerhard, unlike Ducasse, believed that the dreamworld could achieve a density that would one day take on form. The doors would open, swinging inwards, and something marvelous would enter. This was the reason for his effect on people, why they found him so attractive. He heard his neighbor continue the lecture:

"If a woman appeals to you, then you must openly pursue her. This is not only allowed, it is expected; it's one of the rules of the game. In love, man and woman hunt each other. The huntress is always pleased when she sees that her arrow has struck home. It convinces her of her power. The man must show he has been hit, must respond—that's part of nature."

Ducasse increased his benevolence. A smile passed over his ravaged face.

"You will be successful. But only a fool would pride himself on it. After all, everyone is successful who believes in himself and knows how to seize an opportunity. That is why you so often see men who are poor and ugly taking rich and beautiful women to be their wives. Now that society is ruined, there are no boundaries here either, no more forest preserves and closed seasons. The open hunt is one of our basic rights."

From an early age this had been his, Ducasse's maxim, and he had made a royal killing. Not all his relatives had approved of the match, and all of them had seen in it a mésalliance. His father had warned him: "When honor can be bought, the hour of judgment is at hand." That was the standpoint of an age that had run its course, touching, but irrelevant. These monarchists without a king, grands seigneurs at whose door the sheriff could knock any moment, lived in a world that had become unreal, like knights after the invention of gunpowder. They still had no idea of the new method of wielding and enjoying power. And hadn't they come, one after the other, confidentially, after dark, to ask him for greater or lesser sums of money? Practice and theory. At any rate, one enjoyed much more freedom since aristocracy had become just an agreeable way of life.

As for Gerhard, he was listening politely, but with only half an ear. The language of hunters was foreign to him. Even as a boy he had been fond of shooting and good at it, hitting the clay pigeons at every angle from which they were sprung. But when, on an excursion to Monte Carlo, he was supposed to take aim at live pigeons, he had been seized with horror. He sensed that Ducasse was recommending advances of a lower order. There was something statistical about it. The proximity of the sick man began to oppress him; he would gladly have taken his leave.

On the other hand, he felt at ease in this room, through whose curtains the autumn sun was falling as through a red lattice. He had the urge to be alone with his innermost feelings. As so often, he had awakened again that morning with a sudden surge of happiness. He felt then as if he were striding through the depths of a forest, where the air is easier to breathe. When people met him, they appeared stronger and simpler, more important. And they were always good. Or rather: he saw them in the perspective in which they were good.

Irene seemed perfect to him—like a work of art, but here was movement, here was life as well. If works of art were alive, then artists would be gods. He saw a divinity in this creature, who at the same time was natural. Perhaps this is how the ancients came to perceive animals as divine and worship them.

Gerhard had already seen the Countess at his aunt's salon, but he recalled this only as he would a shadow that was now transformed into light. He sensed her eyes resting on him—did she remember him or perhaps feel even a little sympathy towards him? He hardly dared imagine that she would consider him worth a conversation. He would fail: the mere possibility terrified him. On her table was a splendid bouquet of roses. Gerhard scarcely heard Ducasse next to him resume the conversation, which had now become a monologue.

"Haven't you ever observed on the train how a man and

a woman strike up a conversation? And how they then get off together at the same station?"

At this moment the Admiral and his daughter got up; they passed by the table. The Admiral nodded, the Countess smiled.

"What did I tell you, you lucky man? You should send her some flowers."

Gerhard blushed. "That would be too forward."

"On the contrary—it would be a sign of savoir vivre and would be felt as such; you may be sure of that."

Ducasse shook his head. It was hard to get this simpleton moving. But it would be worth it; that he could foresee.

"Leave that to me. Give me your card and you will see that you have made the Countess extremely happy."

And seeing Gerhard still hesitating, he added: "You can also pay for our luncheon, although I invited you, and I shall select the most beautiful roses for you. Forgive me for having been such a poor companion. Ah! When I was your age and had your appetite, I was more amusing."

11

Kargané stood in the doorway, peering half irritated, half amused into the room. It smelled overpoweringly of perfume; Irene had thrown a set of crystal bottles against the wall; the scents had intermingled. The Captain thought: "Perfume should be smelled only on the skin." That was also one of the reasons why he doubted his wife's instinct. She used "Ambre" after getting up and "Chant de Châtaigne" at night—the hint for the morning hour in bed before tea was brought.

During their marital disputes, Irene would tear up or smash any objects she could get her hands on—the more valuable, the better: hand mirrors, tortoise shell fans, lacework, gold watches; she had a predilection for expensive destruction. This did not displease Kargané; it was a sign that the storm was subsiding. There it was the rain, here the tears; he needn't worry about leaving her alone. He loved to devote his time to women, but only as long as they didn't bore him.

He stood there silently, pressing his beard with his left hand against his chest. This was a gesture he had picked up from the effendis—and actually more than a gesture: an attitude with which he maintained his dignity and kept his mouth closed. An effendi doesn't respond to questions he doesn't like, and above all in his own house. Those were European vices.

He took pleasure in the feel of his beard, as if his hand were resting on the bluish fur of an animal. It was already shot through with the first silver strands. They did not bother him. The fear of aging was another European prejudice. Life grew more enjoyable with the years; experience played an important role—with age, a man not only felt he was enjoying, he knew it. It was like participating in the theater of life at once as actor and spectator. In his youth, a man shot his bolt too impetuously and had ideas that brought headaches rather than joy.

Now the fad of beardlessness was encroaching from England—another sign that things were going downhill. These clean-shaven faces reminded him of the eunuchs who served in the inner recesses of the palaces in Cairo and Constantinople. If he, Kargané, wore a beard, then it was not, like his father-in-law and his set, in order to hide something, namely an insipid physiognomy—on the contrary. His mistresses found the beard repulsive at first, but soon learned otherwise.

Tolerating these scenes belonged to his liberal accoutrements. He knew their course from experience; they were repeated a number of times and then gradually abated. In the long run they could only show who was master in the house. Of course, Irene was not pliable; in front of guests he could not even feign harmony with her. She had just been terribly spoiled. She was nothing but trouble, and her dowry was being dissipated on extravagances. Half of the insolent creatures serving here were superfluous; there were neither masters nor servants anymore.

This time she had been particularly furious—his absence had outraged her not only because of its duration, but even more on account of its intensity; she sensed that she had become unimportant to him, even tedious. Like most women, she possessed an infallible instinct independent of facts—an immediate insight into the extent of his infidelity. His denials were of no avail, and lying had become a form of politeness.

Following his return he had been unusually distracted— even when he possessed her. He had mingled strange words, strange gestures, even strange manners with his caresses. This was more than just a sign that she was beginning to bore him. These voyages to the Levant had become indispensible to him like a bath that restored virility. But there, too, he saw signs of decay, traces of bad conscience, Western influences. This process could develop final nuances; the effeminate Sultan who ruled on the Bosporus was their prototype. But here, too, the last hour had unmistakably sounded; the triumphal march of universal platitude could no longer be checked.

Kargané believed that he had been born a hundred years too late. Something irretrievable had been lost with the sailing ships. He hated the engineers who were now on the rise, hated the Suez Canal and the steamers, although he had commanded armored vessels and had mastered their tactics. Since Tegetthoff, encounters between men on the high seas were no more.

Kargané often said that it would be a good thing if a man could ride along with the development of technology as though he were on an excursion, getting off where he felt most at home. "I'll stop where they fire cannonballs at wooden ships." He would gladly have taken part in the Expedition to Egypt. He had a predilection for the brief stylistic period known as "retour d'Egypte": winged, dark-headed sphynxes, Nubian busts, candelabras in front of hieroglyphic curtains. After his departure, he had considered converting to Islam; he was still toying with the idea today. There was no better way of coming to terms with oneself and the world. But how long would they continue to hold out down there?

His glance fell through the window upon the framework of the Eiffel Tower, now nearing completion. He had almost forgotten Irene, who was lying with her face on the pillow. She rose and walked towards him in her dressing gown.

"Are you still here? You know how much your face disgusts me."

She was glaring at him full of hatred, screwing up her eyes into narrow slits and tilting her head back. Her pupils contracted, intense little dots, as though darting tiny flames.

"We're not through with each other yet, my fine Count. You won't be able to show your face in Paris when I'm finished—you can depend on that! Then you'll have time for your shepherd boys. You certainly know the company that suits you."

She burst into provocative laughter.

"I'll pay you back in your own coin, and with the greatest pleasure—this very day, believe me!"

The smile vanished from Kargané's face. He clasped his hands behind his back and cracked his knuckles. For a moment he had thought of tearing off her trappings—that was a reliable method, but she no longer meant enough to him for that. And then there were the servants, the utterly outrageous lack of privacy in a house like this, where someone was always ready to give notice, perhaps even call in the law. Here more effective methods were called for. A meal together was out of the question; he turned on his heel. "I'm dining at the club."

Downstairs in the drawing room he lingered for a while

at the window; a cigar would be good right now. The room was on the mezzanine; from the vestibule there was access to a terrace, which in the summer, almost like a Mediterranean patio, afforded a pleasant sojourn.

The house seemed out of place in the quarter; it was modeled after the palaces that had been preserved in the Marais: two forward wings enclosed the *cour d'honneur*. The drawing room recalled the saloon on transatlantic ships: mahogany, sturdy furniture that held up to sea travel. The paintings on the walls, originals or good reproductions, fit in with the rest.

Seascapes depict either the sea in its various states or its interplay with human activity, usually scenes of disaster: shipwrecks, battles, burning ships. Though a Breton, Kargané felt and lived like a Mediterranean; the sea with its monsters was more unfathomable in its translucent calm than during storms. He had no feeling at all for Turner and his mists; he considered him colorblind.

A lot of light with sharp reflections and neat contours as in Vernet's harbors, danger and terror captured in a single instant as in the *Slaughter of the Tuna*. Nelson at Trafalgar on board the *Victory*, Tegetthoff at Lissa, leaning on the mast, saluting the enemy admiral. His favorite painting was *The Sinking of the Kent* by Gudin.

Kargané recalled that Irene had once said to him: "You're a philistine—*what* is painted is more important to you than *how*." Perhaps this was true—his literary taste as well was less attuned to style than to facts.

"After all, even a piece of beef can be painted in

completely different ways. But I can still tell whether it comes from an ox or a bull. Instinct counts more than taste. And that from a woman who's not even . . ."

He interrupted himself. The footman was escorting a messenger with a bouquet to the servants' entrance. "Yellow roses—*jaune fait cocu*. Another one of these giddy actors or some other good-for-nothing . . . to be delivered personally—in a minute Mercury will return with the answer." Rage welled up in him.

He decided to cancel the club and, before leaving the house, went to see Mauclerc in his office.

12

"Isn't posthumous fame a strange thing—almost as if you were playing the lottery? For instance, did the unfortunate Guillotin, as a physician and humanitarian, deserve having his name linked forever to a beheading machine? It's so unjust. And in other names, like Simon and Onan, an ephemeral deed endures as the quintessence of infamy. And this Xanthippe? For a notorious loafer probably just the right wife.

"Then take a lucky devil like Maréchal Niel, whom I knew well, though he was a bore. There was really nothing duller than those generals of the Second Republic, who fade from memory like shadows—imitations of an imitation. He was the commander at Sevastopol, one of the stupidest massacres ever, and promoted the introduction of a particularly murderous rifle with a zeal that was worthy of a better cause, worked himself to death doing it. Everything, including his book on the Crimean War, has sunk into well-deserved oblivion. And what happens? Along comes an ingenious gardener and christens his most magnificent rose 'Maréchal Niel.' Now there's a graft that took: while the historical sprig wilts, this one burgeons in gardens to mythical splendor. From now on, this name will wondrously evoke fragrance and color. That's the way it is—how few have earned their fame."

Ducasse loved such puzzles, with which he filled in the gaps in his time, as at this moment while standing in a flower shop. It had not been easy to find, since most of the shops were closed on Sunday afternoon. Besides, this one was more a covered stall next to the Madeleine, and there was not much of a selection. "Maréchal Niel" was usually available, but today it was nearly sold out. Of the yellow variety Ducasse had in mind, there was only one bunch left, with slender buds and curved red thorns that gleamed among dark-colored leaves. Next to it was a blood-red rose whose covering leaves had scarcely opened yet and were glistening with tiny droplets. Ducasse found them too ardent for a first greeting. After hesitating a while like a chef pondering over a seasoning, he decided in favor of the yellow bouquet. He had it sent to the Countess's address and enclosed Gerhard's card.

The sight of the roses had a calming and invigorating effect on Irene, as if she had drawn a deep breath. She felt appreciated like a heroine presented with flowers on stage. Kargané must have caught a glimpse of the bouquet—that was fine with her. She read Gerhard's card and smiled. Aha—the little blond today at lunch—some sort of diplomat. She had already noticed him at Frau von Zimmern's and had recognized him immediately. There was something unreal about his features that prompted out-of-the-way moods; it almost seemed odd that he went around dressed like everyone else. Despite the heated discussion with her father, her eyes had been drawn to Gerhard again and again and had lingered upon his face as though they found repose. He must have noticed—yes, without a doubt he had noticed. This bouquet was his way of thanking her. It came just at the right moment, as a great assuagement. She turned the card over and saw that there were a few sentences written on the back.

"Madame, the days when a man could offer assistance to a lady he found saddened and distressed are, alas, long gone. But even today a mere sign, a word might suffice. You looked so unhappy. May these roses cheer you up a bit."

Ducasse had thought up this text and worded it in such a way that he would be able to answer for it if need be: what might be added by an older, well-meaning friend, although he was sure that the question of authorship would not arise. He knew of Irene's penchant for extravagances and had also hit upon the perfect opportunity—an explosive moment.

Irene had been endowed by nature as well as society with all the gifts that ensure a happy existence. If things were clearly otherwise, then it was because some of the cogs were turning faster, with more abandon than was suitable for the whole.

There are several reasons why excess is antagonistic to happiness and fulfillment. Quite aside from the fact that it does not always spring from vitality, it has an inherent tendency to destroy pleasure. You can enjoy a banquet in a pleasant atmosphere, amidst the harmony of cheerful conversation. But when personalities are on hand who thrive on strong drinks, noise and bickering, a malaise takes hold, as though one were feasting on rough seas.

The erotic coupled with excess, as in Irene's case, is inauspicious. Whatever causes a stir, attracts the curious, and betrays a taste for scandal can only make matters worse. Linked to this was a kind of failure which plagued Irene and was inexplicable to her. At moments like this, when she was moved, on the one hand, by furious indignation and, on the other, by a sense of emptiness and futility, she had often sought encounters, had even tried to force them, and these had led invariably to an embarrassing or ridiculous conclusion. It seemed then that her partner would become alarmed and withdraw; the game lost its meaning. It had even been known to happen that externals intruded and aborted the affair. These adventures resembled a labyrinth whose paths led without fail out of the erotic domain.

It was no coincidence that she was attracted to Gerhard, for her provocative personality insured that she sought after timid partners. Kargané was much too strong for her. Even during their conflicts she remained dependent on him.

There had been similar altercations after his previous return; these had led to the affair with young Coquelin, who was much sought after as a romantic stage lover. She had admired him many times in *Manon Lescaut*, *The Two Orphans*, *Around the World in 80 Days*, and other plays—not only evening after evening, but also at the dress rehearsals at the Porte Saint-Martin. This actor represented a type one might call the perfection of prettiness; he had a doll's figure and moved very gracefully—in short, she could have eaten him alive. She had added to the number of his worshipers, had sent him flowers every day, and finally, in a state of mind much like today's, had sent a frantic note.

They had seen each other briefly two or three times and then arranged to meet in a little hotel behind the Madeleine. It was here that the young man's adventures would reach their climax, which most of the time was also their conclusion. Unlike the plays he appeared in, they did not lead to repeat performances and jubilees; often enough they did not go beyond the premiere. That explained the choice of location—an impersonal hotel with luxurious appointments.

This quarter had its unique charm until it was cut up by the large boulevards. Behind the church, which looked more like a pagan temple, there was still something left of it, as on a tiny island. The great stream of traffic flowed past it; craftsmen's ateliers and shops without display windows enjoyed a small but loyal clientele. Then there was the proximity of the market and its bustling energy. This was the right neighborhood for discreet assignations. The small hotel "At the Golden Bell" had only four or five tables, which were carefully kept separate from each other, and several rooms on the second floor. It was run by Madame Stephanie.

The elegant impersonality of the place was not likely to disturb young Coquelin, since he was the model of the impersonal lover. This was one of the reasons for the fleetingness of his adventures; he was like a piece of fruit that melts on the tongue with a most agreeable flavor, but scarcely leaves an impression. For him, personal matters were more liable to hamper as an added inconvenience.

What bothered him about the accomodation was more the scantiness of the decor. He was touchy about everything having to do with furnishings; never was the mere intention or any need allowed to show. He was of delicate, discriminating taste, and easily peeved. His ideal was the enchantment that occasionally, though seldom, in the theater overcomes both actors and audience—the magic of a second, artificial nature. He sought the perfect partner, with whom he could chat and move about in pleasant rooms as if slightly inebriated. Like all who strive for an ideal while obliged to represent it by the merely human, he did not cover his costs; the books did not balance.

He came closest to his wishes in private pleasures. Thus he never used his apartment near the Rue d'Anjou for rendezvous. He had arranged things there to his own liking—simply, in the English style, and without the exorbitance that was to be found everywhere nowadays. Here he would spend his mornings, after he had prepared his tea with scientific meticulousness, memorizing his parts, as he walked back and forth between two mirrors in which he rehearsed his gestures. On the wall was a handsome portrait of Kean, whom he revered and strove to emulate, although he had nothing in common with him other than perfection—and here only in drawing-room roles.

It is rare good fortune when heart and soul so completely harmonize with the profession that one can no longer speak of work. The play becomes life, and life a play. Here the young mime benefited from his extraordinary memory. When he had read a new play in bed in the evening, he would be able to recite his part the next morning while shaving as if it had been written expressly for him; learning was no problem for him. Perhaps one could have argued that this very facility was a sign of emptiness, but wouldn't it detract from a talent like this if the characters were more profound? In keeping with this was the criterion that Coquelin applied to an erotic encounter: it was expected to satisfy on a higher plane, which meant it had to be unproblematical.

In Australia there is a species of arboreal birds whose male ingeniously decorates its mating ground with flowers, feathers, and colorful stones, so that once everything is arranged to perfection, he can bring the female of his choice there. It was in this manner that Coquelin decorated his apartment for the queen of his dreams, collecting whatever he tracked down at the antique shops on the right and left banks. As noted, the furnishings were simple, but if a fabric, a painting, a piece of furniture was wanting or had to be replaced by something better, he spared no pains, went to any length to obtain it. Since the Petersburg tour he no longer had financial worries and could afford to spend on a grand scale. Thus, like a good painter, he would apply tone upon tone to the ensemble. Occasionally, when he inspected his work, he would imagine the raptures of a congenial spirit to whom he would reveal this little world for the first time. This was most agreeable.

Meanwhile he would not tolerate women there, except an old woman who did the heavy work in two hours. Whenever he received a male visitor, which was seldom enough, he would ask him to refrain from smoking. His way of combining order with amenity would have made him a good eighteenth-century abbé, and he would have gone far.

Irene was the partner least suited for such inclinations. In fact, he had sensed this as soon as they had passed from the language of flowers to words. Alone with this unknown woman in Madame Stephanie's little suite, he had been overcome by the feeling that he had fallen into a trap. The woman was restless, abrupt, overwrought. She sprang from an oppressive silence, during which she looked him over with penetrating, greedy eyes, into a sudden gale of laughter. In the midst of it, she made remarks which depressed him, like: "One gets the impression you can't get along without a prompter."

Coquelin wondered if she was in her right mind. He had a foreboding that the adventure was about to take a most disagreeable turn and sought to extricate himself. Later, he himself was astonished at his trepidation; after all, meeting extravagant admirers went with the profession. There was something else involved here as well: the immediate threat from a person who was not only harmful herself, but who also attracted harm from the outside.

In his mounting anxiety, he had suddenly left the room and asked Madame Stephanie to inform the lady that he had taken ill and gone to a doctor. After this rather unmanly exit the flowers had stopped coming. A letter bristling with insults had actually relieved Coquelin, since he had feared that the affair would drag on, or even that the Captain might go after him. Like most actors, he was superstitious; he would rather have broken a mirror than have repeated the encounter.

Although not the only disappointment of this kind that Irene had experienced, it had a particularly violent effect, a particularly bitter one. She had had such high expectations. There was still fundamentally something of the child in her—an impulse that made her desire a toy impetuously and then destroy it.

Both came to the fore when Gerhard's flowers arrived and she was holding his card in her hands: her anger at Kargané, her desire to cut him to the quick, and the memory of the humiliation she had suffered at the hands of the actor. An intense joy took hold of her: she would settle both accounts, make up for everything, and this very day. She also knew where. In spite of everything, the rooms in the shadow of the temple had appealed to her; the spot was discreet and convenient. She had gone back two or three times, though with little more success. The hostess knew her—if only, as Irene thought, anonymously. That simplified matters.

13

The mild, almost summery day was followed by a cool evening. It made the fog rise that was slowly spreading from the river through the streets. It moved from the bridges like a carpet up the hill. The light of the stars shone through the haze and then vanished completely. The sounds also grew fainter, fuzzier. One could hear the horses' hoofbeats and the rumbling of the carriages as they returned from the theaters.

Fog lends cities an intimate note, a chamber tone. During the day it attenuates forms and subdues the sun's glare. At night it transforms the quarters into one large house in which corridor blends into corridor and room into room. There are temperaments who abhor such weather and others whom it draws onto the street. Among the latter are not only those who love the confined and intimate, but also all who like to go about in disguise. Solitaries who have spent the day immersed in bizarre reveries are now up and about like bats in attics. Lovers embrace each other as beneath cloaks of invisibility. Lepers savor the pure air. Beasts of prey roam their trails, while in the ports foghorns are heard.

Gerhard had been waiting for a half hour behind the Madeleine at the indicated corner. The florists had long since shut down their stalls, but a fragrance of mignonettes was still hovering above the refuse, mingling with the fog. Though Gerhard was exhausted, he was wide-awake and full of anticipation; after taking leave of Ducasse, he had gone for a long walk through the woods beyond the Bridge of Saint-Cloud.

At home he had found Irene's letter; it had taken him by surprise like a shout, although he was not particularly astonished. He was always expecting something miraculous; if it came true he would be happy, but with the feeling: "I knew it." So Ducasse had been right when he made the suggestion with the flowers—things were probably simpler than he, Gerhard, imagined. There were certain formulas one had to know, secret instructions for grown-ups.

The proposed hour could not really be called improper, for impropriety is a concept with leeway. Rather, Gerhard inferred from it that something extraordinary was afoot— one of those tests that would allow him to prove his devotion, courage, and loyalty that he had so often dreamed of. It would have been even less of a surprise if he had been summoned to an uncanny place—a catacomb, a cemetery, or a dark forest.

He had read the hasty lines of the note again and again; he knew them by heart. "Whether you can help me? O yes! How well you guessed it—it touched me like a miracle."

So she had sensed what had moved him. Tacit understanding—there was nothing more beautiful, not even poetry. Thus flowers might be swept by a gust of wind— flowers for which a ray of light acts as messenger. But what could he do for her? How did she happen to think of him with his inexperience? But goodwill could make up for a lot. He would shed his blood for her.

He felt radiant and warm, in a kind of drunkenness. The fog enfolded him like a cloak. How lucky he was to have run into Monsieur Ducasse; that couldn't have been a coincidence. He had clearly misjudged him. Ducasse might well be one of those messengers who deliver the keys when you are standing in front of a locked door. Soon everything would change, that was certain. And suddenly, inexplicably, a shudder passed through him. He saw the lamps, around which the fog thickened into yellow spheres. Objects drew closer to him.

A carriage stopped behind the church, then light footsteps came toward him. His heart began to pound; it had to be the Countess. He felt a pang of terror as if silk were tearing; the hour had come. He wasn't certain if he was only dreaming, but the dream was beautiful.

It was she. He felt her hand on his arm.

"It's good you've come. I had scarcely dared hope for it."

She pressed his hand.

"What weather! All the cabs are taken. Still, I would have come sooner if I hadn't wanted a carriage with a white horse. I thought: if I find a carriage with a white horse, he'll wait for you—I know that's silly, but you see that I was right."

She laughed. He saw her eyes through the light-colored veil she was wearing. Her figure was hidden beneath a fall coat; she was holding a delicate umbrella in her hand. Now she was speaking to him in an urgent whisper as if afraid of eavesdroppers. He was her confidant, her co-conspirator. He said:

"I thank you for having thought of me, although I am unworthy of it."

"You can be trusted, or else I wouldn't be here. Call me Irene—your name is Gerhard, isn't it? I saw you at your aunt's. But are you going to make me stand here on the street when you've given me a rendezvous at midnight?"

The question perplexed him, it frightened him. The encounter had been the luminous point which he had been moving toward like a butterfly—he had not thought how this would develop. Without doubt he had put her in a dangerous or, worse still, an equivocal position. Somebody might come by any moment, and there was a good chance it would be somebody she knew. Half the city knew the portrait of her by Odilon Redon. Gerhard began to tremble; he felt guilty. But what was he to do? He did not even dare to answer.

Irene, too, seemed frightened. She clutched his arm more tightly, as if seeking protection. It was almost as though she was gently pushing him backwards. He felt the pressure of a door at his back, which, yielding, opened without a sound. Again Irene squeezed his arm, but this time with tender reassurance; she caressed his hand. A wave of confidence emanated from her. She was clearly on the right path.

The time had come to hide, for footsteps rang out on the pavement; they heard voices, laughter getting closer. They went in; the door slid shut behind them. They were safe.

14

The door to the "Golden Bell" was only opened at dusk; it was then left ajar until after midnight. Madame Stephanie's guests did not like waiting on the street; they preferred to enter discreetly and leave the same way—this had to be taken into account.

But the entrance was not left unguarded. As long as there were still guests in the restaurant, Madame Stephanie would sit enthroned behind a little desk where she added up bills, collected money, and supervised the personnel. Here a round window had been set in the wall, a bull's eye that commanded a view of the corridor. Hanging in front of it was a little bell that was activated by a chord whenever the door opened. One really had to have very good ears to hear it, but then Madame Stephanie had excellent hearing. She could distinguish the faintest sounds in her house.

Besides the door to the hotel, there was also the one that gave free access to the restaurant, then the back door, which opened onto the market and was left open during the day for deliverymen and employees on their errands. It was locked at night, but there were certain guests who preferred to use it. Madame Stephanie let them in herself and locked the door behind them. It was even said that several customers had their own key to this back door, but this was a rumor.

The house with its several doors had an organic structure, like the pictures of the heart one can study in textbooks of anatomy. The circulation of blood through the various auricles, ventricles, and valves is predetermined; only a catastrophe can change its course. It was much the same in the "Golden Bell"—here one could enter the hotel corridor from the restaurant, but not the other way around. There were guests who knew the house only as a restaurant, and others who knew it only as a hotel. After eating and drinking downstairs one could take a room upstairs, but not come back down into the restaurant. Further orders were served in the room. What was requested upstairs from the kitchen and cellar went up the back stairs—there were no exceptions. Madame Stephanie had her reasons for this. The front stairs were only dimly lit and nearly always empty.

The running of the house was also organic inasmuch as it was based not on rules but on long-standing practice, and followed a set routine. Madame Stephanie had a steady clientele and personnel with long years of service. In such cases, direction can become a kind of game; a glance, a hint suffices. The business went like clockwork and was a gold mine. Its guests were by no means niggardly. Madame Stephanie insisted that painters and people of that sort be kept out; as for actors, they had to have a reputation like the young Coquelin. This rule did not apply to actresses; here beginners predominated.

People felt at home at Madame Stephanie's. She was a pleasant person and, though in her riper years, still rather attractive. Her beauty was quiet, like that of a nun; it was due mainly to the regular proportions of her figure and her face, which were accentuated by a mysterious smile and a soft contralto. That gave her an impersonal quality which, like the portrait of an old master, was looked upon with sympathy.

Humans love the Recurrence of the Same—above all, when it evokes and renews the memory of hours of fulfillment. Thus, in the varied existence of her circle of friends and benefactors, Madame Stephanie had become a figure with an aura of tradition. She was guardian, custodian of hours long faded, which flared up again the moment one set foot in the vestibule. The air one breathed there was redolent of thuribles in which incense has been burned for decades.

This effect was strengthened by the fact that Madame Stephanie hardly aged. She was still the same person they had known at the time of the vernissage; at most, darkening imperceptibly like a painting. There she stood, the same as always, with her mysterious smile, in the frame of the dimly lit vestibule. Year in, year out, she wore dark clothes, whose only adornment was a necklace of ivory pearls. This went well with her complexion, which was marked by a pallor such as castigation produces in cloisters.

Order and discretion ruled in her domain. She knew every one of her guests, but never would she have acknowledged one without being called upon to do so. As for order, it is often compared to light and is similar to it also in the sense that it only becomes discernible through disorder, as light through darkness. Order is less important in the barracks than on the battlefield, in the harbor than on the high seas. It is true, Madame Stephanie's establishment flourished in complete secrecy, but all sorts of things could happen if one loosened the reins.

Women's energy is stronger, though less apparent, than men's. It is penetrating, less volatile, more commanding. It is more flexible and yet harder than the famous blade of steel. But like steel, it has not possessed this virtue from the beginning, but acquired it by being chilled in cold water. So it was, too, with Madame Stephanie. She had to go through her own bitter experiences, what for some time the people in her native city of Mantes had called her offense. But now she was known as Madame Stephanie there as well. The title had its full value.

But it had been hard back then in the maelstrom of the capital; after shipwreck came the threat of drowning. Of the recruits who enter the barracks there every year, perhaps one out of a hundred makes the rank of officer. It is the same with the female contingents whom, year in, year out, the provinces sacrifice to the capital as to a Moloch—very few achieve the rank of a Madame Stephanie. Just as the soldier is promoted, above all, by distinguishing himself in the front line, so it had been here: she had begun in a particularly difficult position as waitress in one of the well-known places of entertainment on Montmartre. Here she had soon been found trustworthy and put in charge of the bar—a dangerous distinction.

A bar that fulfills its purpose, that is to say, offers the best to the guests as well as the host, is like an altar on which offerings must be made to Dionysus as well as to Mercury. That requires two conflicting abilities on the part of the employees, namely, they must be able to stimulate and also keep track of business. It is in keeping with the spirit of the institution that activity approach the level of an orgy without being allowed to go quite that far. Otherwise the profit would be consumed in festivity. It would go up in smoke along with the fire. That is why there have to be stations from which the consumption can be watched and supervised, and one of these stations was occupied by Madame Stephanie, then known simply as Stephanie.

Crowds of habitués and travelers from all over the world remembered her this way. Even then she wore dark, low-cut dresses with flashing buttons and lace trim at the front and on the sleeves. The skirt was puffed out by a "vertugade." At that time she had gold-blonde hair as was required. Night after night she would stand amidst the uproar, behind the long bar in front of the mirrored wall. In spacious rooms draped in red, people were dancing, drinking, singing, and laughing. The colorful whirling motion beneath the large chandeliers rose up to the loges veiled by smoke. The music was scanned by the popping of champagne corks, rent by screams of peacocks and parrots. The grand festivities were repeated every night, and there was not a foreigner of any prominence who did not render his offering there. Here one could see Stephanie, standing from nightfall to the break of day, her arms propped up casually, always smiling prettily. The table bore large bowls of magnificent fruit and batteries of bottles with gold and silver necks, which, when opened, ran with foam. Here was someone ordering, over there a disagreement, here a regular customer to be greeted by name and there a shout to be parried, all in good cheer. Thus performers are able, with a smile or pleasant gesture, to hide how difficult the number is.

But what was going on inside this cheerful person's head? Many who would have gladly kissed her would have been astonished to find out. They would have found numbers as in an adding machine, nothing but numbers and names, or physiognomies that were interesting only in so far as they were connected with the numbers. This brain was as reliable as the Bank of England, or at least as that of a croupier who has turned gray in the casino at Monte Carlo. It knew debit and credit as if they had been engraved with steel, however wild the merriment.

In positions like this, there are two possible deviations in regard to figures, the upward and the downward, both of which are detrimental. There are the possibilities of forgetting, of overlooking, of wrong addition and subtraction. These are mistakes that can happen to the best of us, especially in the surge of excitement, quite aside from other perils. Moreover, there are matters of discretion such as credit and the like. There are temptations more numerous than St. Anthony's. There are also gratuities. But perhaps it will suffice to report that Stephanie was not only able to consolidate her position from year to year and make herself respected, but that she also laid aside considerable sums of money. Besides this, she had good connections.

Success like this required, as we said, two completely contradictory abilities. Stephanie possessed both to a rare degree, and this accounted for her success. In our day we hear a lot of bad things about the divided soul, and also much that is stupid, since the split, as one of the world's fundamental principles, is manifested no less in good than in evil. From success as great as Madame Stephanie's, we might infer a contradiction in her gifts and qualities that leads to surprising results. Therein lies the power of the unexpected. Everybody knows that a joke goes over all the better, the more seriously it is told. This is the reason why we rarely find a good comedian. Likewise, a cat that wants to catch a mouse will not jump about wildly, but appear the very image of tranquility. And in the same way, Madame Stephanie was bound to flourish in a world that was devoted to love and joyous pleasures. She had the pleasing appearance, the quiet conscientiousness this world demands. Behind it was a vigilant, calculating mind, aided by the sure eye that abstinence confers.

15

The rare days on which Madame Stephanie traveled to Mantes to visit her relatives, who for some time now had held her in high esteem, or on the days when she had her attacks, she was replaced by her housekeeper: Mademoiselle Picard, dependability personified.

The seizures recurred regularly, with severe migraines and abdominal cramps. During these crises, the right side of her otherwise ivory-colored face turned a fiery red. Then, despite her energy, Madame Stephanie had to strike sail and take to her bed. That was a great burden, even if it rarely lasted longer than a day. There was no remedy for it, though her physician, Doctor Besançon, who lived right nearby, had made every possible effort. He usually prescribed warm compresses and opium drops and when he took his hat and cane never failed to make the remark: "I should write you a prescription for a healthy young man, Madame Stephanie." Knowing that such quips irritated his patient, he immediately added: "I mean you should get married." Madame Stephanie would then reply: "You'd better get out of here, Doctor."

The doctor, as a seasoned bachelor, was fond of provoking women with risqué jokes; he found it cheered them up. The brief interchange had taken place today in the same spirit, although the migraine had been particularly violent. It grew even worse toward evening when the fog set in. There was a stirring inside her body as if spirals were contracting, then unraveling again. The right side of her face was burning, the left was ice-cold. Now the fever was unbearable, and now the fits of shivering.

Madame Stephanie lay in her bedroom. The house had been built the previous century after the manner of Genoese villas: with a first and second story and a mezzanine for the servants. The lower story was reserved for the restaurant, the upper one for the guests. The mezzanine had a low ceiling, the walls were slanted. That makes bedrooms even cosier.

The drops had already taken effect. They were beneficent. They produced a condition superior to sleep—a kind of flight that carried one gently over flowering meadows. But the flowers were more beautiful and less fleeting than roses and lilies, as if an angel had painted them and brought them to life. In their contemplation, pain and time disappeared.

But did time really disappear? It could just as well have stood still. Every now and then, in the glow of the night lamp floating in a glass of water, Madame Stephanie glanced at her clock. It could happen that after she had lingered endlessly on the flowers scarcely a minute had elapsed. This was bewildering—time shot past like an arrow and simultaneously stood still. One was standing on the bank of the river and at the same time amidst the rapids, in the center of the wheel and at its spinning edge.

Endless dreams were a great luxury for a woman who was on duty day and night like Madame Stephanie. She was well aware of this in the intervals in which she peered at the clock. And today she was especially uneasy, since Picard was bed-ridden as well. Her left arm was badly swollen; the doctor wanted to wait until tomorrow, then he would make an incision. How often had she been told to be more careful carving the meat. When they had duck, she would pierce the birds with a fork like an expert. But she worked too fast. And a puncture like this is worse than a cut.

Outside the church clock tolled; no doubt the one in the Rue Duphot. Twelve strokes could be faintly heard through the fog. Was the back door securely locked? Madame Stephanie was not easily frightened, but the back door was the weak spot in her house. Although the market closed down early, there was always something going on around it. There were big dogs, drunks, and lovers loitering there in the corners. Over on that side one had to watch out. Maybe she should have locked up, which, of course, had happened only once before, at her niece's confirmation.

Joseph was in the restaurant, so no need to worry there, but for the rooms there was only Bourdin to help out. Bourdin was an indomitable servant, but one could not present her in public, except, perhaps, when someone had broken a glass and she appeared with her broom and pail. More than that could not be expected of her.

Madame Stephanie made an effort to get up, but she fell back exhausted. Once again she soaked a piece of sugar with the brown drops and let it dissolve in her mouth. It had a bittersweet, rather repugnant taste. Tomorrow—this she knew from experience—she would be fresh and take charge as in her best days.

16

Bourdin, who was carrying things from the kitchen, heard the bell ring. She sighed and went into the vestibule. She

was not the type to be pleased when given added responsibility. How to scrub the stairs, how to clean a pot until it
shines like gold in fire, that she knew, there no one could
tell her anything. But the slightest demand on her initiative
made her recoil. She then saw a mountain of difficulties
looming ahead of her. Yet if a superior was present, like
Mademoiselle Picard or the mistress, she would have faced
the devil himself. It is for this sort of person that medals for
long and loyal service are intended.

Her appearance was hardly inviting. Her hair fell in gray
strands over her forehead; on her mouth a cut had left an
unsightly scar. There she stood, next to the brightly colored
plaster blackamoor who lit up the stairs with a lamp,
suspicious, apprehensive, the embodiment of the equivocal
situation.

The door was open, and fog was coming in. In the
vestibule stood a lady accompanied by a boy. The lady was
holding roses in her hand.

Gerhard realized that it was up to him now to take
charge, but he did not know what to say. That made the
situation even more embarrassing. Finally he heard Irene
say:

"We have some things to discuss and do not wish to be
disturbed. Open up a room for us."

Bourdin regarded her closely. Madame Stephanie knew
at first glance whether there were rooms free or not. She
insisted on irreproachable clientele, and those coming in off
the street could not fool her. But how was poor Bourdin to
know the right thing to do? She could see that this was a

fine lady; somehow the voice seemed familiar to her. She said:

"We only rent for the whole night."

Irene gave an irritated laugh. She lifted her veil:

"But surely you will allow your guests to leave when they please?"

Now it began to dawn on the servant woman: this was the lady that the young actor had brought. They had had trouble with her, but here one did not pay for smashed china. She had come two more times—but only, as Madame Stephanie put it, for a "flirt." There was no doubt about it: it was the lady from number Twelve. Bourdin now knew what was what.

"Madame, your suite is already occupied. I can give you the one next to it—it's just as good."

That was a blunder that neither Madame Stephanie nor Mademoiselle Picard would have made, and Bourdin immediately paid the consequence:

"You tramp—I don't know you."

Irene pounded the floor with her umbrella and turned to Gerhard:

"Don't just stand there as if all this didn't concern you. Give her some money at least. You can see who you're dealing with."

That was the tone Bourdin understood. She knew now that the lady had "good blood," as hotel personnel would put it. After taking the money, she led the guests upstairs. There she opened the door to a kind of drawing room. On the mantelpiece a lamp with a red shade gave a subdued, pleasant light. Bourdin asked whether she should also light the chandelier—an offer which was always declined. But they did want a fire in the fireplace. After that she opened the door to an adjacent room, which was left ajar, and showed them the bell for room service. Then she withdrew. The couple was alone.

Irene stepped in front of the mirror; the light was favorable to her. She had already removed her cape. Her voice now sounded much friendlier, ingratiating:

"How awkward you are. But of course that was an outrageous creature. To think the house has a good reputation. You don't think ill of me for asking you to come here, do you? A friend gave me the address—I could only see you in complete secrecy or not at all. Besides, I have to leave right away."

The room was almost exactly like the one in which she had had her tryst with the young Coquelin. Only the painting above the fireplace seemed to have been switched—but again a Deveria: a couple embracing with a red curtain in the background: a subject of modest intimacy. Its character was underscored by a bronze plaque with the inscription "Bride and Groom." Beneath it the name of the painter—it was the less gifted of the two brothers, who was known for his remarkable range of subjects. In addition to mawkish devotional pictures, which were popular in private chapels and boudoirs, he also produced fiery pornography. There are those who secrete his cross-sections of bordellos, in whose rooms little red and black figures cavort. Of course this was unknown to Madame Stephanie. But her predilection for this painter may well have involved the subliminal.

They were now sitting facing each other at the gas hearth.
The logs were made of perforated copper, along which
flickered tiny bluish flames. For the first time they had the
leisure to look at each other—the way one looks at pictures
and photographs. Irene had had a lonely childhood. Whenever she had been given a new doll, she withdrew into a
corner to play with it to her heart's content, without
witnesses or spectators. The strong feeling of possession that
had seized her then was what delighted her now.

This beautiful creature's misfortune stemmed from the
fact that emotionally she still lingered in childhood—in this
respect Gerhard was her kin. It was a meeting of precocious
children, not of adults. When Irene had seen the Captain
for the first time in her father's house she realized that things
had grown serious, without any transition. Until then she
had not known how much power the eye could have. She
had discovered this while conversing with Kargané—
alarmingly, as if a pirate ship dropped its disguise and let its
cannons flash. How was it possible that these eyes transformed themselves into a pair of lights which cruelly and
with shameless knowledge penetrated her being? And still
more incomprehensible—she had answered on the spur of
the moment, had said yes to his question with the same
knowledge, the same shamelessness. It was the flame that
follows the flash of lightning. With that everything was
settled; there was no resistance. In effect, he had taken

possession of her like a pasha; the compulsion was stronger than all the fetters of the Orient.

From the very beginning she had rebelled against this domination. She could be conquered, but not vanquished. On the contrary, each new attack strengthened her resistance, which intensified into hatred. And yet her jealousy increased along with it.

How different was the idol which she preserved within her and to which she sacrificed in her dreams. She had come closest to it when she was sending young Coquelin flowers and fruit every day like a shepherdess who lays down her gifts before an image. Rapturous awe would seize her when he came on stage and transport her beyond reality. One could have heard a pin drop in the theater when, with nimble grace, he stepped up to the footlights. Irene had to close her eyes—this was the epiphany; her sacrifice had been answered.

She sought to forget what had happened then. Her difficulty lay in the fact that she expected real things from the ideal, and from the real, transcendence. This is a common affliction, and entirely human—only in her case it had intensified to the point of mania. Thus she vacillated between expectation and disappointment.

While she was looking Gerhard over, he merged with the young actor as he had been before he disappointed her. Now she would bring the matter to a happy end; she would not miss Kargané anymore—on the contrary, she too was going to travel, and with Gerhard. First she would give him the appearance that appealed to her; he would be docile enough. She could already see him stepping onto the terrace, while downstairs the horses waited. She felt a sudden desire to stroke his hair, to show her affection. She took his hand.

"Gerhard—may I call you that—I'm so glad you came."

For Gerhard, who led a pure life of dreams, it was as if he was awakening to a higher reality; how light and yet how precious this hand felt. This was an enchantress that had come to visit him. He was going to hear wondrous things, but he wished that time would stand still and everything would stay as it was.

17

He did not know how long they had been sitting there, with her hand resting on his and his hand in hers. To grant timelessness is the essence of time. Here their intimacy was complete, they felt safe. Gerhard was happy, and the next thirty hours of his life would be dominated by the memory of this happiness, as if he were paying the price for it.

Suddenly Irene withdrew her hand from his and pointed to the door, as if she had seen something frightful. And Gerhard, who followed her glance, took violent fright: he saw a face peering into the room.

Madame Stephanie had had the upper panel of all the doors replaced with panes of glass, because that lit up the corridor and made the work easier. Of course, they were frosted; through them one could not see into the room, nor out into the corridor. The possibility that someone might press his face up to the glass had not occurred to Madame Stephanie—that could not happen in her house. Of course, then one would be able to see it, as did the two lovers now to their horror, even through the frosted glass.

It was hardly likely that the observer could make out what was going on inside. But he did see the lamps, the fire, the shadows of two people at the fireplace. Nor was his face any more distinct. It was as if a pale fish were sucking on the glass. They saw it as one of those grotesque faces that children carve in pumpkins and then light up with a candle to frighten other children—as a fetish-head.

The specter was only visible for a second, yet a terror issued from it as if it were transforming the room into an evil chamber and charging it with guilt. Then the light went out in the corridor. Irene had jumped up: "Oh, that's horrible—lock the door!"

Upon entering, she had noticed that he had failed to do this. Young Coquelin had not made that mistake; of course, she had not known how much at home he was here. It was getting eerie. She put out the lamps.

As Gerhard approached the door, there was a noise outside, indistinct, no words were audible. A suppressed giggle, footsteps like someone dancing on the carpet—faint, but the commotion could be heard through the door. All that within seconds, like the crackling of a fire from which, suddenly, a naked, blood-red flame shoots forth.

"No, let go of me!"

Immediately after that a scream that shook the building to its very foundations, a scream the likes of which Gerhard had never heard before, but which he immediately understood. It flashed like lightning through chasms in whose depths the knowledge of it lay hidden. It tore open the fabric. It was the scream of a person being murdered, being murdered with a knife.

Then it fell silent, except for a stamping as if a giant were striding past—or was it his own blood that Gerhard heard pounding in his ears, the mowing rhythms of his heartbeats? But he had to help; he slid back the bolt, which he had already locked.

The door sprang open without his touching the handle; it yielded under the weight of a body that must have been kneeling or sitting in front of it and now fell halfway into the room—with a groan that made the heart freeze. That was no longer a sign of life, no sound from realms in which pain can be felt.

18

Gerhard knelt at the head of the dead woman, touched the still warm forehead. Here help was no longer needed, no water, no linen, neither priest nor doctor.

The room was lit up by the bluish glow of the fireplace. The light was dim in the corridor as well. It was the first corpse he had ever seen. She was wearing only a thin chemise and a red slipper on her left foot. The body gleamed like marble up to the hips, then came the ghastly destruction, as if the image of a goddess had been steeped in blood.

Gerhard did not know what was due the dead, yet he sensed that this body was in need of protection; he could not simply abandon it. He had not noticed that Irene had disappeared. Mortal terror had made her freeze and then given her the strength of a wild animal. Seizing the only possible escape, she had leapt over the corpse, leaving her hat and coat, and fled into the corridor.

This had happened while Gerhard, in a complete daze, had heard his blood pounding. The scream had been followed by a deep, riveting silence, as if life itself had been paralyzed by it. Then the "Golden Bell" grew animated like a sinking ship. Windows opened on every story; there were screams for help. Outside whistles could be heard, and murmuring as if a crowd was gathering.

There was commotion on the stairs; doors were slamming. From the room across the way, a gentleman with a short, gray beard appeared in his shirt sleeves; the suspenders arched across his chest. After he had regarded the corpse with senatorial gravity, he withdrew.

On the ground floor there was an exchange of words.

"I'm a knight in the Legion of Honor."

"I don't care if you're the President of the Republic!"

When the police arrived, a group had already formed and was standing in silence around Gerhard and the dead woman. Madame Stephanie, though more dead than alive, was rushing around the house and seemed to be everywhere at once; she realized that nothing more could be saved. This was the end of the "Golden Bell," its ruin. She had thrown a sheet over the corpse in order to cover up the abominable sight, but alas, nothing could be kept secret here. As in an ineluctable nightmare, she stood staring at the red stain which was steadily spreading out from the center. There was no way to conceal anything, not even by rolling granite over the outrage.

PART TWO

19

Etienne usually arrived at the Police Criminelle, where he had been on duty for several weeks, between nine and ten o'clock in the morning. The offices were located in the Palais de Justice; to reach them one used the entrance on the Quai des Orfèvres.

He would already have spent an hour on horseback, in the woods if the weather was good, in a manège of the Military Academy if it was raining. Then he would have a cup of black coffee and take a walk along the bank of the Seine. That was very pleasant, especially now that the leaves of the tall poplars were turning. When he was a bit early, he would continue on a few steps to visit the Sainte-Chapelle—not because he was religious, but because he felt that it bolstered him. There, amidst the blue and gold of faded images, he sensed the reflected splendor of a life that had disappeared from the armies. Moreover, the centaurian activity of riding demanded a counterbalance.

Etienne had been trained in a regiment whose colonel had gone through MacMahon's school. Whenever an officer was recommended to the victor of Magenta for a command or a promotion, the general would lay his hand on the dossier and ask: "How does he sit his horse?" On the basis of this he made his decision. That a Minister of War could be thrown during a parade, as happened later, would not have occurred under him.

One would sooner have gone on duty after a sleepless night than without one's riding practice. Horsemanship was observed as a rite. It had also become second nature with Etienne and indispensible like habits of hygiene or ritual. He found it beneficial, and not only for his mètier. This, of course, demanded self-assurance and unreflecting, spontaneous authority. But the effect went much further and was more comprehensive. Etienne saw proof of this as well in the fact that the melancholy which often stubbornly plagued him gave way to high spirits. A problem that had seemed insoluble when he got out of bed would no longer give him any difficulty. This must have been a result of the optimism produced by an early morning ride in the woods or a turn around the hurdles. That reduced the phosphorous.

On the other hand, this optimism would also provoke misgivings, since he was rarely satisfied with himself. At times he was depressed by the suspicion that this kind of health might be damaging him intellectually. After all, problems could not be taken as easily as hurdles and ditches. What good did it do to leap over the fine lattice of light and shade and not see the labyrinths traced in the sand? The net of doubts and contradictions was easy to rend like spiderwebs, and yet the risk was greater than breaking one's bones in a fall. The lighter the weight, the heavier the responsibility.

Etienne had chosen his profession voluntarily. It had

afforded him many pleasant hours, if not the satisfaction he
had hoped for. Being a soldier today meant something
different than in the days of the king who had built
Saint-Chapelle, something different even than under Na-
poleon. One soon realized this, especially in a garrison like
the one in Nancy, where there were hardly any diversions.
Duty was tedious and demanded little effort. The evenings
alternated between the Hotel "Walther" on the Place
Stanislas and the "Viennoise" in the Rue Michottes.
Compared to this, the year in North Africa had been like a
drink of spring water, although they had often nearly died
of thirst.

Etienne was overcome by moments of estrangement
when he would step outside himself and with astonishment
observe himself in this or that situation. Such a not entirely
favorable endowment presupposes refinement. It leads to
reflections as in a cabinet of mirrors.

Today, too, it had amazed him that he, Etienne Laurens,
at this moment was walking through the entrance on the
Quai des Orfèvres. He was looking down on himself from
above as if he were passing through the portal of an anthill.
What did all this activity have to do with him, these swarms
of people milling about on the banks of the river and on the
island? The haste, the earnestness with which they were
rushing to and fro could only be explained as an optical
illusion. Either *he* was mistaken or everyone else was.

And what sequence of ramifications had it taken for him
to see himself at this very moment in front of this entrance?
First, there was his entering the army nearly twelve years

before, and then the fact that he had been transferred from Nancy to the Deuxième Bureau.

And then, once again, a branching off, a command within a command as it were, this role as guest of the Police. If one stopped to think about it, and Etienne had a penchant for brooding about questions that touched upon the problem of free will, one could grow anxious; one might see oneself as a plaything of fortune. And perhaps the branch from whose outermost tip he was now dangling had been worm-eaten from the beginning. Once again the thought occurred to him that he had chosen the wrong profession.

On the other hand: if one assumed that not chance, but necessity was at work here, was it any better? What did all these appointments mean? No doubt that they felt him to be a foreign body which they wanted to reject—gingerly, of course, and even honorably, for in the performance of his duties he was above reproach. There he was even more thorough, more methodical than most; he was a good instructor, an indefatigable drillmaster who also appeared in the barracks when his name was not on the duty roster. And he was not a stickler; the men liked him. Off duty he was actually more correct than good form required. The colonel was partial to types who got themselves into serious trouble and whom he then with great difficulty got off the hook. Daredevils aroused paternal feelings in him. "He has passed the hussar test," was one of his inveterate sayings.

No, it was different with Etienne: he conformed only halfway; a character with whom one could not find fault, but whom one also could not warm up to. Perhaps he judged himself too favorably when he ascribed this to his intellectual superiority, which at the same time was a shortcoming in that it detracted from the esprit de corps. The troop's function, after all, was to gain the upper hand during the attack.

The sort of remarks Etienne let slip among his comrades went far beyond their grasp. They were greeted, at best, with embarrassed silence. Experiences like this made him cautious. His attempts to adopt the current expressions had also failed. Incredible what a fine ear they had in this regard. Their hearing was sharper than their intellect. They were able to hear what was behind the sentences, and the result was that they and Etienne felt ill at ease with each other. There was something of a different race about him. Even when he did something better, he did not do it right. In the evaluations, his weak point was the personal comment, the "cote d'amour."

Nonetheless, there were exceptions. These were rare enough. Among his superiors as well as among his comrades and subordinates, Etienne came across individuals with whom he made friends right away. The first sentence would reveal a secret understanding, and sparks would fly as though steel was striking against flint. This was followed by a rapid exchange as in a game of badminton. Encounters like these were like wells on a journey through the desert. Evidently there were two breeds—one that formed figures according to the rules of a higher zoology, and another, sparsely distributed breed of the mind.

It would be nice—this was one of Etienne's favorite ideas—if the latter held the reins. But society was obviously ordered after a different model. This was apparent not only in the army, where the rugged always prevailed. If intelligence influenced the plan at all, then certainly not through intelligent individuals. Actions were supplied with just the amount of knowledge they required, and better too little than too much.

When individuals happened to have a superior insight, then it was no doubt superfluous, extravagant, fruitless like a pollenated flower blooming in a winter garden. What could it mean that in spite of this individuals always appeared whose thoughts, feelings, inclinations went far beyond historical necessity? The World Spirit might perhaps tolerate them in its castles as poor relatives who could not be of much use, but nonetheless as relatives whom it would now and then let in on its plans. Occasionally it climbed from the ground floor up to their attic.

These were the kinds of combinations that had antagonized his comrades in Nancy. If the intellectual bent was not exactly considered treason, it was nonetheless viewed suspiciously. This improved when the others livened up as well, for instance, after drinking a bottle of Pommery.

How gratifying it was, on the other hand, when one had found a partner who responded to intellectual combinations and took the same pleasure in them. They would sit together in the garden or in a room in which there was no lack of books. They smoked, the teapot was replenished. There were mental architects; with them one executed imaginary designs. There were daring spirits who ventured far out into the unknown. There were systematic minds, visionaries, polemicists. When they were silent, the room became even more charged. A ray of sunlight warmed the century-old spines of the books, one heard the rain rustle in the trees, or bluish flakes fell in the twilight onto the pointed gables.

In Nancy there had been one of those adventures which might be described as the preying on society of two intelligent individuals. Etienne was glad that it was over. For this reason as well, he had welcomed his transfer to the capital. A blank page in the book of life lay open in front of him; he felt free for new encounters.

20

That he had gotten to know Inspector Dobrowsky here was a gift of fortune. It did not come entirely as a surprise to him. The depression that had befallen him when he took up his assignment was an indication. He knew from experience that on the eve of such changes he was overcome by paralysis—even in the hotel room where he unpacked his suitcases for his leave. Everything seemed bleak and hopeless. But he also knew that this would change come morning and that the new location would prove salubrious. From the severity of the depression Etienne even inferred his future high spirits. They followed each other like ebb and flow. Perhaps this was the reason why death was necessary.

It was here on the quay that he had come across Dobrowsky. This was a windfall; it transformed the posting which he had regarded at best as a barren stretch of road to be put behind him. The successive assignments had awakened in him the feeling of being on a downward course, although they were rather considered marks of distinction. There was no one in Nancy who would not have been glad to change places with him.

He had not felt at ease in the Deuxième Bureau; the atmosphere was strained. And that was not all—on the very first day they had stuck him in the Statistics Section, where he had to translate German documents although the place was swarming with Alsacians. The office was located in the Rue Saint-Dominique; its name was a cover for the Intelligence Service.

The matters dealt with there, as Etienne sensed immediately, had only peripherally to do with soldiering; by nature and technique they were closer to police work. The candor that is customary among soldiers was missing. Every hunter is shaped by his game. In the Deuxième Bureau the uniform served rather as a disguise. Their vigilance was directed toward the invisible, guileful enemy whom they had to combat with his own methods. Absolute mistrust was mandatory, a mistrust that spared no one. It also defined the nature of camaraderie. Etienne sensed that obliging manners had a different meaning here, that they concealed something and that every conversation was conducted as if a third person were present. After a few days he had already been given to understand that somewhere in the army, perhaps in the office itself, a wolf in sheep's clothing was hiding. By sheep's clothing, they meant the uniform.

The officers were undoubtedly more intelligent than the troopers. But their activities had two sides: they were cavaliers in the morning when they appeared in the woods on horseback, but it was quite different in the evening when, in dark glasses, they met their agents in churches or obscure corners, entangled in repulsive transactions. They dealt with characters whom they despised.

Major du Paty was the only one whom Etienne had seen a few times outside of work. He had attracted him as a mind who combined tradition with cultivated tastes. But it was difficult to tell what was genuine and what had been acquired by reading. Had his ancestors really used expressions like "Sword and Altar"? Perhaps, but then not with this literary elan, the pathos of the "Libre Parole." As a passionate Wagnerian, the Major attended the Bayreuth Festival every year, although they frowned upon officers of the Deuxième Bureau traveling to Germany.

Their fondness for each other had already waned when Etienne was assigned to the Police. This suggestion had been made by the Commandant of Paris, a commander who would have fit in during the period of Rome's decline. That the Deuxième Bureau employed police agents now and then was a matter of course in cases that were taken up by the army as well as the police. Only when it was unavoidable did one resort to this collaboration, since, as

Du Paty put it, "it makes a big difference whether a conservative or a Masonic agency conducts the investigation." As a way of reducing this mistrust, the Commandant thought it would be advantageous if an Intelligence officer were to serve for a while with the Police.

The Minister had given his approval, though for different reasons. The Paris police had developed methods whose knowledge was indispensible to the Secret Service. For years Bertillon, a criminologist of European renown, had been working there as chief of the Identification Office. His measuring system for exposing criminals was famous everywhere.

The order was received without enthusiasm in the Rue Saint-Dominique, but it had to be obeyed. That Colonel Sandheer, the officer in charge there, chose Etienne was a form of sabotage: it meant that the information would benefit an officer whose employment in the Deuxième Bureau was only temporary. But things had been done by the book.

At police headquarters, they first sent Etienne through the various sections. Each chief had the natural desire to present his domain to visitors in a favorable light—so it was with Gonod. Furthermore, he did not burden Etienne with instructions. Thus it happened that he stayed on in the "Commission des meurtres", the section for capital crimes. This could be justified inasmuch as the entire police force is called in for the investigation of a major crime. But the real reason was to be found in the friendship that had grown up between Etienne and Inspector Dobrowsky.

This sympathy at first sight was all the more strange since the two men differed strongly, not only in character, but also in their appearance and habits. Etienne had been exposed from childhood to surroundings in which great importance was attached to dress. At home he had already been given thorough training in this. His colonel, liberal in moral questions, supervised uniform and posture as a true pedant. In all the corridors and riding rings hung large mirrors in which one encountered one's full-length image as in fashion houses. Over the years this led to a second conscience with respect to outward appearance, which one heeded as if about to appear for inspection.

The Inspector, on the other hand, had obviously never given any thought to whether the articles of clothing one wears should go together. He wore suits from the rack, impossible neckties, shirts and collars upon which the lye from laundries had tested its causticity. That did not bother him. His mind was on other things when he threw on his clothes in the morning. The intense reflection he was caught up in made him adopt the bad habit of biting his nails. They were always gnawed down to the nub as well as being stained from the juice of countless cigarettes.

Thus they made a strange pair when in the Café de la Régence, the classic meeting place of chess players, they sat facing each other at the table. Etienne, hoping for closer acquaintance, had suggested these chess games, which were then followed by conversation; and apparently the Inspector enjoyed them too. Moreover, he was a good player who could have become a master if he had had sufficient time for it.

Etienne had the leisure to observe his new friend while Dobrowsky, biting his nails every now and then, pondered his moves. He was not easy to classify. He had one of those faces which have become much more common since the invention of the railroad: many races leave their traces in it and become anonymous.

Dobrowsky had been born in Cahors, in the very street in which old Gambetta had had his general store. He had begun his career as a policeman in Marseille; in the Old Port he had won his detective spurs. There he had acquired his profound knowledge of everything concerning the dregs. In Paris he had quickly risen in the ranks. He was Mediterranean in origin, in his predilection for garish colors, his Genoese business sense, and also in the mixture of bad manners and cordiality. But there were other elements as well—a kind of amoral, omnivorous passivity. All this gave him his broad scope. He could suddenly switch from the almost clairvoyant sensitivity of a medium to intense activity, like a big cat ready to pounce; this made him especially suited for manhunts. It became quite apparent when he played chess. "You should play chess sitting on your hands." This was meant figuratively, for Dobrowsky would smoke, drink coffee, and bite his nails. This betrayed the pain and self-torment of an indecisive mind. Etienne had less the impression of an opponent capable of subtle combinations than of a player before whose eyes countless possibilities pass by like ciphers on a moving tape. Suddenly he would stop the tape and make an astonishing move. That was the danger. Besides intelligence, there was also something of the intuition of a lottery player who guesses the winning number. It was conceivable that among millions of innocent passers-by it could pick out the culprit.

Dobrowsky was small in stature; he had the brownish complexion by which a doctor recognizes certain liver disorders. His skull was enormous and covered only by a dark tinge, like the down of embryos that disappears while in the womb. This matched his sensitivity to the most subtle impressions. It was strange that a person who was able to weave together perception and judgment like silk threads should have so little taste. But Dobrowsky did not have an artistic temperament. He would never have been able to judge the value of a painting, but he was competent as to authenticity.

When he had contemplated the chessboard long enough, the plasticity of his face changed in a surprising way. He took on the piercing look of a bird of prey. Etienne had the impression that his gaze, having rested for a long time on the surface of a burning glass, now came into focus. This occurred again in conversation. There it was a stroll along thickets out of which now and then a bird flew up or a deer suddenly bolted. After such surprises Etienne grew more cautious in their conversation. At the same time he felt the burgeoning of sympathy and respect. He had had many comrades, but never a friend. At first he was bewildered, embarrassed as one who is in love and must hide it from his family. That passed with growing intimacy.

After they had played several times in the "Café de la Régence," where the Inspector did not feel quite at ease, they moved over to the "Four Sergeants of La Rochelle," a small place located near the Bastille. Dobrowsky lived nearby. He loved this section of the city.

When they had finished two games and had had a few drinks, Etienne accompanied him as far as his front door, which he never entered. He knew very little except that his friend was married. Usually, the Inspector then walked Etienne part of the way back. They followed the old street, which, beginning with the Rue Saint-Antoine, leads into the western quarters. Sometimes they would take one of the narrow streets with such strange names as Rue de Petit Musc, and head toward the Seine. There they had their best conversations, when the lights were reflected in the water, but the Inspector preferred the streets that bustled at night. He had an insatiable appetite for faces, for figures drifting by—returning exhausted from work or decked out for pleasure, also bent on crime.

On these walks they traversed the different social climates that are divided by the equator of the Rue Royale. They came across harlots and touts who where looking to make contact, an old man creeping along as if on his last walk, a woman crying, a gentleman in a fur coat who asked them for a light for his cigar, and young people in all stages of drunkenness. The kaleidoscopic change of figures seemed to have something intoxicating for Dobrowsky; he would linger at places where the crowd clustered together, congested in bottlenecks, or formed fleeting groups. Again and again he touched Etienne's arm and asked: "Did you see *him*?" Then he would converse with a hawker of lewd pictures, with an Italian roasting chestnuts in a doorway, or would follow the reeling path of a drunkard.

It might also occur to him to suggest a walk through the maze of streets just east of the Bastille, which branched out around the Rue de Lappe. There he knew the courtyards, the corners and blind alleys, the dance halls and dives where the professionals discussed their plans and disposed of their booty.

"Not only heroes live in the shadow of liberty," he had said as he led Etienne past the Column of July in the moonlight. "There is no word as voluminous as the word liberty—it can embrace the entire world. A truly fascinating word."

These nights always offered new images, which were scarcely coherent, but left a vivid impression. They appeared to have been painted meticulously in lurid colors on black lacquer. The manner in which Dobrowsky led these expeditions contributed to their hyperreality. He saw the people in their occupations and passions more intensely than they did themselves; he saw them as connoisseur. It often seemed to Etienne as if he had tasted a piece of the serpent which, once consumed, enables one to understand the language of the animals. Dobrowsky assumed the bearing of a hunter who knows that there is game close by. He did not enter any premises without first informing the uniformed agents who always patrolled in pairs here. One was venturing onto territory in which the social contract was no longer acknowledged and where circumspection was called for. But Etienne felt safe in his friend's company as with an experienced climber on a dangerous bluff.

Dobrowsky took him to the big dance halls, where violent scenes could always be expected, but only small fry were to be caught. The Apache reveals himself the moment passion takes hold of him; he offers a big target. The Inspector had studied a number of these careers. They were like chains in which short and long links alternate: brief spans of freedom with years of imprisonment. This inevitably ended in prison, in a bloody fray, or on the scaffold. He had sympathy for these fellows, who were mostly good-natured, but they did not present him with a challenge. "Those are cases for Delavigne," he would say; with this remark he was alluding to a minimum of criminological acumen. Delavigne, a lanky youth, was a candidate in Dobrowsky's office, and Etienne had the impression that he kept him there for his amusement or for the sake of contrast.

The pure Apaches, recognizable just by their clothing, hardly figured in the Inspector's favorite reading: the dossiers in which unsolved cases had been slumbering for years. He took them up again and again, compared them, sought the signature of an unknown perpetrator, to shed light on the style of the crime, the method of working, the field of activity, the rhythm of the forays. There were individuals who only went to work when the moon was full.

"Just as a painter, a novelist always returns to his motif, his subject, and an early work already prefigures his development, so it is too with criminals, who, for the most part, strictly adhere to their characteristic pattern, their *poncif*. With a bit of experience, one can say, when called to the scene of a burglary: that was Jacques or Louis, as one might say looking at a painting: this is an Ingres or a Cézanne."

"Those are bold comparisons. So you assume that there are expert performers, an elite among these people?"

The Inspector had answered Etienne's question affirmatively: "That is doubtless the case. In fact, the hierarchy is determined by the degree to which intellectual weapons are brought to bear and make crude acts of violence unnecessary."

He had gone on about this at great length, as he liked to do on his walks. According to him, the aristocrat among the criminals could be recognized by the fact that he abstained from violence, above all, did not kill. Combinatory power could attain high levels, it could reach zones in which the law loses all control of it. The theories about crime were inadequate because they limited themselves to the symptoms, that is, to the damage caused to society. But there is a difference between this demonstrable damage and criminal potential. This potential has its abode in evil; it is possible that it never leaves its den to appear as crime. But just as, according to Heraclitus, the concealed harmony is greater than the visible, so too is this secret domain of evil more dangerous than the sum of all the crimes we perceive. No court of law takes cognizance of this.

What astonished Etienne about such expositions was that they went far beyond the requirements of a policeman. They reminded him of his own situation in the army. On the other hand, they conveyed a contentment and sense of leisure as if the Inspector were only involved in what went on around the Bastille as an amused spectator. Thus a head forester might inspect the game's watering places and feeding areas during the closed season. After the manner of gamekeepers, he did not want too much unrest developing there. "One must also make concessions to anarchy; someone who tried to punish everything would only clog the safety valves."

21

Dobrowsky would also introduce Etienne to one or the other of his clientele in order to provide firsthand proof of his theories. One evening, as they were sitting in the "Four Sergeants" among the petits bourgeois who were playing dominoes and drinking wine, he directed his attention to a thin, neatly dressed customer who was sitting by himself reflecting over his glass.

"You seemed astonished recently at my comparison with Ingres and Cézanne. Here you see a master in his trade. Just as there are painters and sculptors who toil over a work for a long time, which they then exhibit and sell for a high price, this man—his name is Leprince—is no less carefully planning a great coup from whose take he hopes to live comfortably for two or three years. Of course, he's already recognized me. If you want, we can go over and sit with him for a while."

In this manner, Etienne made the acquaintance of a courteous, middle-aged gentlemen who spoke well-deliberated sentences in a pleasant voice. Evidently, the sympathy Dobrowsky felt for him was mutual. The comparison with an artist did not seem quite apt to Etienne; this melancholy, yet businesslike gentleman reminded him more of an engineer, or rather: of a traveling salesman in technical articles, like those he had met on several occasions and in much better establishments than this. There is an aristocracy among them too: men who have time and money. This depends on the wares they sell, and the choice of wares is in turn dependent on their connections. Someone who takes neckties from door to door always remains on the outermost, arduous rings of circulation. He does not even dare dream of a commission as another might chalk up for himself after a fine lunch. Such lucky fellows can be found on board ships or on the Riviera, where they spend months in comfortable idleness. They are cultivated, good partners in conversation. Business is of no interest to them.

This was the sort of life Leprince led. The Inspector was familiar with his habits. He also knew that for each of these pleasant periods Leprince would acquire a new girlfriend; he preferred brunette actresses, who should be neither too young nor extravagant and who never had an inkling of his profession.

Leprince received them at his table with a melancholy smile. Dobrowsky inquired about his health and about his plans.

"Are you going to go on one of your lovely trips again?"

"Not the way you might think, Inspector—that's over with."

"I'm delighted—really, I'm glad to hear it. But my question was not so indiscreet as you suppose—I too am happy when my work is done."

They both smiled as at a *fable convenue*. Then they talked about Lisbon. Some years before, Leprince had committed a burglary there that became famous. He could not help feeling a bit flattered and smiling when the Inspector recounted the details to Etienne. In a luxurious side street of the Avenida da Liberdade were two jeweler's shops, whose owners, as a safeguard, had installed a modern system of bright lights that stayed on all night. In addition, the display windows were not only covered with a grille, but the jewelry was removed from them as well and locked in a safe overnight, which was also lit up very brightly. As if that were not enough, a watchman walked back and forth between the two shops. Nevertheless, Leprince managed to open one of the safes, which brought him not only a stock of mounted and unmounted stones, but also a considerable sum in banknotes.

To accomplish this, he had, in the brief intervals of the watchman's absence, obtained impressions of the locks. Then, with the help of the duplicate keys, he had paid the shop a quick visit, solely for the purpose of photographing and measuring the safe—this had to happen within seven minutes. Perhaps the photograph could have been taken through the window, but not as exactly.

The material obtained in this way had been used by Leprince to construct a kind of firescreen or paravent, whose front bore the enlarged picture of the safe. For his final and actual break-in, he had placed the screen in front of the safe so that it hid him while he was working. He tricked the watchman patrolling outside just as the painted curtain of Apelles had tricked the experts. Within two hours Leprince had opened and emptied the safe. Then he left the shop with the booty and did not forget to lock up again, as is proper.

Dobrowsky added a remark about ingenuity. On its higher levels, it could be recognized not so much by the fact that it overcame obstacles as by its ability to utilize them and integrate them into its plans. It sailed with every wind. Thus in this case the circumstance of the extraordinarily bright light had been used—first for the snapshot and then to mask the welding.

"All the same, the matter was brought to trial, though some years later—the sale of the precious stones was the weak spot here. Even with perfect work there's no avoiding all the hitches—or do you think differently, Leprince?"

"Theoretically, I suppose."

He had said this after some hesitation. The Inspector regarded him benevolently as if he had heard the word he had been waiting for.

"Isn't that so? In theory the best plans succeed, and that is why they should remain in theory. In practice mindless chance intervenes. If everyone knew that this chance disguises a law, then the prisons wouldn't be overcrowded."

He turned to Etienne: "I have to initiate you into our mysteries, dear friend. And it won't hurt Leprince to hear this either; you see, I've given this subject a lot of thought. To exclude the element of chance one must eliminate the traces, for every deed leaves a trace which chance can attach itself to. But every attempt to wipe out the trace creates new ones. You can take that to be a law. It's the same with lies: to back them up you must come up with more and more lies. And that's why there's nothing easier to dismantle than a contrived alibi."

"That would mean that a culprit is all the more likely to be caught, the more carefully he has gone about his work."

"Correct. Intelligence gets caught in its own snares. He who proceeds according to the rules of his art poses a problem that can be solved. The man in the woods who knocks down and robs the first person to come along is more difficult to track down than the most cunning check forger, who must constantly leave traces, even as a signature. Hence we criminologists are faced with the peculiar fact that the dilettante gives us harder nuts to crack than the expert. My unsolved dossiers just go to prove this."

Leprince had been listening attentively: "Inspector, you're a dangerous man."

Dobrowsky laughed: "So I've been told."

Etienne had noticed that he avoided using the words "crime" and "criminal" in Leprince's presence. He said:

"You should write a book about these things, a manual."

Dobrowsky made a dismissive gesture: "I've got better things to do. But you're right, we need one. In our profession the practical predominate, mostly crude minds as in the military, if you don't mind my saying so, Capitaine. Among a hundred generals who manage to win a battle, there is hardly one that can explain the principles to you."

He added: "Such a manual would have to start with the simplest givens: time, space, causality. The culprit has the choice of hour and place; above all, he has the freedom to decide whether the crime should be committed or not."

Then turning to Leprince, he continued: "That's what I mean by freedom, freedom in its full, creative sense, which we police never attain. To be sure, this only holds true for the conception and its mental games—the poetic aspect of the crime, as it were. As soon as it has been committed, the picture changes. The culprit forfeits his freedom, and his pursuers now have time, space, and facts in abundance. And they are numerous—many dogs are the death of the hare."

He rolled another cigarette with his stained fingers and after pressing and tapping it began to smoke with visible pleasure.

"You see, Leprince, you had seven minutes' time to introduce photography into the profession. My colleague Vatel needed seven years to track down one of the pieces of jewelry that had vanished at the time. In doing so, he hardly left his office. He's indolent and lacks imagination, but he has at his disposal a leaden backside and an exact list of all the jewels that are being sought. You wouldn't believe how primitive our methods are."

He interrupted himself and asked: "There were two opals of unusual shape, if I'm not mistaken?"

"I can't remember. Those are youthful escapades one forgets."

"Yes, I understand. Opals bring bad luck, as they say. By the way, pearls are supposed to be very much the fashion now?"

"Pearls and emeralds too, but the preeminence of diamonds is still unshakable."

"But they say that the supply is growing."

"That is unimportant as long as wealth is increasing, nor does it apply to solitaires, which always maintain their price. Their value rises with the profit and scarcely diminishes when it falls. But I'm afraid I'll have to be going now."

After the waiter had given him his hat, coat, and umbrella, and Dobrowsky had shaken his hand, he politely took his leave.

22

Although it was already late, Etienne and Dobrowsky continued their walk, which took them with a few detours along the Rue de la Roquette. The contours of the houses melted into the fog that was rising from the river. From Père-Lachaise wafted the scent of chrysanthemums and withered leaves. The Inspector said:

"There's a back room here where the comrades of the

murderer who's to be guillotined at dawn carouse through the night; an excommunicated priest says a mass and absolves him *in articulo mortis* when the sun rises."

Etienne returned to the subject of Leprince:

"You've really opened my eyes to the hopelessness of such an existence."

"How true. Those are the consequences of expertise. If there was a break-in tonight at the Brothers Fontana or at Verer, his house would be searched, at the latest, tomorrow morning. But in London or Rio de Janeiro he would be no better off. The telegraph is as detrimental to his profession as it is for diplomats."

"And he would certainly do better in a respectable profession."

"That would have no appeal for him. His destiny—not to say, his mission in life—is jewel theft. Only the stolen diamond completely satisfies him; that is an archaic trait. I can even imagine a quickening of it."

"You mean, if bloodshed were involved?"

"Yes—but Leprince is a gambler, not a cutthroat—essentially a peaceable man. Someone meeting him on the street wouldn't think he was capable of his extravagances."

They had turned into the little Rue Saint-Sabin; the Inspector stopped for a moment to light another cigarette, which he had rolled in his coat pocket. By the light of the flame, Etienne saw that he was smiling. Apparently the encounter had put him in a good mood, like a hunter who has found rare game. As they were turning off the Rue de la Roquette, he rounded out his picture of Leprince with further details and developed his theories of jewel theft.

If the Inspector was to be believed, Leprince was what people call a good soul. He was of gentle disposition, sensitive, good-natured. He enjoyed sojourning in small southern ports like Antibes or Saint-Tropez, where he spent months in modest, but comfortable pensions. There he would fish indefatigably from the cliffs; he was also a passionate stamp collector. Moreover, he had never committed an offense involving stamps. His girlfriends idolized him. Women in riper years who had had their disappointments regained their confidence thanks to him, and felt appreciated for what they were. There were marriage swindlers who were very much like him, and in this field, too, he could have been a great success, if he had been able to bring himself to hurt someone who was attached to him. Not only his girlfriends, also his landladies were thunderstruck every time they heard that he was wanted by the police. They helped him while he was in prison. There he was well liked too. Only with regard to jewels he had remained primitive, undomesticated. Compared to this, what astonished the public—the startling means of acquisition—was secondary.

They were now crossing the square named after Voltaire and had to watch out for the carriages that were gliding past in the fog on the wet cobblestones. Etienne was again amazed at the turns that his friend was able to give his subjects. Each time it reminded him of the departure of a companion who, from the boat they have been sharing, disembarks on an island. The current was opinion, the land was fact.

Dobrowsky now asked whether he, Etienne, had not noticed on occasion how the travelers in the compartment behaved when the train was approaching the border: the zeal with which a dignified old man hid a box of cigarillos and his wife a few ells of lace, and then the unconcealed satisfaction when the coup had succeeded. What did it mean when a millionaire exposed himself to great inconvenience for the sake of a few pennies? It was probably the memory of a time in which, long before states existed, property had essentially been booty, above all, the booty of the hunt. But now it was the State that was despoiler of unlimited personal power. To have triumphed over it, even in a minimal way, was an imponderable but priceless gain. From this perspective, a theory of crime was possible that stood up better than any social or economic one.

But Dobrowsky wanted to keep to the subject of the jewels and asked Etienne whether he could understand the enticement of gold and precious stones and how they practically invited theft? This desire originated deep within; its object was not so much monetary value as the concentration of Plutonian power. Not everyone was allowed, not everyone was able to wear jewels free of risk. In the Middle Ages there were strict rules about this. In those days, not everyone had the right to wear a sword, to add a tower to his house. These were questions of power which, within the economic community, were transformed into questions of money, but this was only a disguise. That is why the open display of jewels still involved a risk, a provocation which glittered from behind the grating of the jeweler's windows as through the grid of a stove. Had Etienne never sensed that atmosphere of vigilance, rapacity, prostitution, and sated contentment smoldering around such places? It was concentrated in the solitaires, whose history has been known for centuries. Hindu deities, princes, great courtesans and billionaires had possessed them; ominous legends were attached to their names. Their actual status was that of talismans; as such they belonged to the royal treasure, to the very substance of the dynasty.

"The great stones, the solitaires, are the quintessence of earthly power. They inevitably produce an opposing power; their ownership is impossible without safes and bodyguards. The greed they provoke is part of the risk taken by the wearer and at the same time reveals what worth he attributes to himself. The greater it is, the greater the danger. What private citizen would dare appear with a diamond like the Sancy, which passed from the treasure of Charles the Bold to that of James II and on its sinister journey was extracted from the corpse of a messenger who had swallowed it? Louis XVI also wore it at his coronation, if I remember correctly.

"That may explain," concluded Dobrowsky, "why our friend Leprince doesn't take up a respectable profession, although it would be easier and more lucrative for him. There is an age-old spur in this way of life, as is the case with our fellow citizens whom you see getting on trains every Saturday with their dogs and rifles. They undergo incredible exertions, tramping through woods and meadows, and if they are lucky they bring home a few partridges.

How much cheaper and easier it would be if they got them at the markets."

"Don't such disgressions go beyond your responsibility and even infringe upon it?" asked Etienne.

"Not in the least—a policeman is obliged to acquire a more intimate knowledge of the criminal than the judge, for instance, or the public prosecutor. His relationship to him is like that of the hunter to his game. He must track him down in the same way, get to know his hideouts, imitate his language, his manners, his appearance. This is an age-old profession. And the criminal can only be apprehended if his mental traits are taken into account as well—I'd dare say: his cast of mind."

"But isn't to understand all to forgive all?"

"So they say. That's another one of those proverbs that doesn't mean anything, a favorite commonplace. Someone who understands everything not only understands the offender, but also the judge who pronounces the sentence and the executioner who carries it out. I'd be more modest and say that I may not understand the total picture of things, but I admire it as a masterpiece."

"So then you think differently than those who say that God cannot exist because this world is a place of horror."

Dobrowsky laughed. "Even if I'm just an ordinary policeman, you don't seriously think I'm capable of such platitudes."

He added: "I am still able to recognize a crisis."

The fog had meanwhile become very thick; the contours of cypresses stood out in the light of the street lamps. Etienne deciphered the name of a street sign: Rue de Repos. They must have arrived at the cemetery. He followed the inspector as in a dream and was hardly surprised when he saw him pull at a bell whose handle was hidden behind a grating. Dobrowsky evidently knew his way around here as well.

After a while they heard footsteps approaching, and a little window opened. In its frame appeared the head of an elderly woman; she was holding a lamp. Behind her a dog was growling. Dobrowsky said his name and was greeted like an old acquaintance. He inquired: "How's your husband doing, Madame Paturon?"

"Badly. He can't get out of bed. I'm sitting up with him now. He's in a miserable way. Robert is outside; he's making his rounds. But won't you come in?"

"No, thank you, Madame Paturon. We only wanted to see if everything was alright. You know that your domain is especially important to me."

"We know, Inspector, and we're grateful to you for it. It's a great comfort to us."

When they had taken their leave, Dobrowsky said: "If the weather were better I would have suggested a walk through the cemetery—very few Parisians know it at this hour. When the moon shimmers on the oriental cupolas and obelisks and covers the paths with silver, one is thousands of miles and years from the metropolis. The great Babylon then becomes so small. But Paturon should be told first, because one might run into him or his assistants when they make their rounds with their weapons and dogs."

"One would think that there is nothing quieter, nothing more peaceful than a cemetery at night."

"That is one of the romantic fallacies. When it comes to crime, the cemeteries are second to the markets and small wooded areas on the outskirts of the city. They have a peculiar atmosphere, a particular attraction for lovers, suicides, and lunatics. Paturon could tell you all about it—for instance, abou˙ the frightful Sergeant Bertrand, a hyena who haunted this place over forty years ago. It staggers the imagination. Paturon had just started at his job. Since then they've increased security. But how about another turn around the wall and going back to the Bastille by the Avenue Gambetta?"

Etienne agreed; they continued their conversation and separated well past midnight.

INTERROGATIONS

23

When Etienne entered the Palais de Justice the next morning, he was immediately struck by the unusual activity in the hallway leading to Dobrowsky's offices. It was swarming with police in uniform and plainclothesmen. Rushing about in their midst were telegraph operators, messengers, court clerks; reporters were crowding in front of the door.

The police number among the institutions that are sensitive to changes in weather. Even if the fog, which had been more typical of a London night than a Parisian one, could account for a certain enlivening of activity, the commotion was nonetheless an indication that something quite extraordinary had occurred. Etienne was not unfamiliar with this feverish agitation from his years in the military. It usually occurred before inspections, and especially parades. The difference was that there it was only a spectacle, here an actual offense. The weapons might be smaller, but they were always loaded, and one was always up against the enemy.

No sooner had Etienne hung up his coat in his small office than Delavigne rushed in. He was supposed to put Etienne in the picture. This was presumably the Inspector's way of getting rid of his assistant for a while. It was a mystery why he had burdened himself with this assistant, who like a poorly trained pointer did more harm than good. Perhaps it was partly because he considered Delavigne unsurpassable in producing commonplaces. One could learn from him in a split second what path should definitely be avoided, and that was already a help.

The inspector, who had a sense of humor, kept the trainee aground as a comic character. In every group there are figures who invite this role and, particularly in public agencies, relieve the monotony of the work. This was largely the case with Delavigne. Like many young people who are much too tall, he distinguished himself by awkward movements, and there were few opportunities for collision that he let pass by. Like Don Quixote with Amadis of Gaul, he had crammed his brain with the Great Pitaval and saw the world filled with criminals. This reading was followed by English murder mysteries, which were becoming the fashion; ever since, he copied the Anglo-Saxon style of dress and deportment.

Delavigne's amusing effect belonged to that type of comedy which is based on the discrepancy between intention and result. The baggy suit with its too-wide collar, the checkered vest, the rectangular shoes recalled in an embarrassing way the costume of Phileas Fogg in *Around the World in 80 Days*, which was playing night after night at the Porte Saint-Martin.

The Inspector took particular pleasure in seeing his trainee engage in a thought process that either produced an absurdity or ran aground in shallow waters. He also enjoyed listening to him on dull mornings complain about his domestic miseries, for despite his youth Delavigne had already married, or rather had been married, by Gisèle, a petite brunette from the South who took him even less seriously than everybody else. Yet while the others found him amusing, he provoked her only to fits of venom. She was given to treating him as a severe creditor treats his debtor.

Gisèle had a fringe of dark fuzz on her upper lip; she loved fish soups and everything else that came from the sea—sailor's fare. The very smell disagreed with Delavigne. Ever since she had taken a girlfriend in, his domestic life had become even more unpleasant, because the two of them joined forces against him. He had been expelled from the bedroom and had to spend the night on a divan that was much too short for him. They had even demanded that on Sundays he serve them coffee in bed. But this he had refused.

Dobrowsky listened to this attentively. Just as there are teachers who cannot enter the classroom without their pupils being instantly provoked to the wildest mischief, there are also men whose wives do not show them the least bit of respect. The former cannot enter into the pedagogical situation, the latter into the erotic situation. That's where the rod would come in handy.

The trusty Delavigne was probably only a trainee in this regard as well. There lay the snag; but there were still other methods for taming the little demon. For a man with Delavigne's ambitions this was in fact a duty. What if he tried showing a slowly growing interest in the girlfriend, doing errands for her, bringing her little gifts? That would certainly be enough to change the situation—if need be, he might risk an assault during which his wife would discover him. That could produce a good effect in a variety of ways.

"But that woman is even worse than Gisèle," replied Delavigne.

"Inspector—those aren't exactly moral suggestions you're making," said Etienne, who had been present during the conversation.

"Do you find it more moral that a man allows himself to be maltreated in his own house by two harridans?"

24

It was Delavigne then who informed Etienne about the murder in the "Golden Bell." The Monday papers had already been distributed hours before, and the news had burst upon the city like a bomb. But as early as midnight there was hectic activity in the Cité.

It was as though they had been expecting this deed, since the news about the woman killer in London had been the subject of conversation for months. It had evoked the mood of winter evenings when ghost stories are told and every gust of wind, every opening door is terrifying. When the plague is raging in distant ports, we first hear dark rumors, then ghastly details, until finally the health authorities report the first case in our own city. They found a dead sailor in a boarding house. This had been expected for some time, feared—perhaps hoped for? Fear harbors strange abysses.

Popularly the murderer was known as "Jack." Now there was only *one* opinion: Jack had shifted his terrain because London had grown too hot for him. The murder in the "Golden Bell" marked the beginning of a new series. Delavigne, too, was convinced of it. "Aha—evidence to the contrary for Dobrowsky," Etienne had nearly said. Nor did the Inspector, according to Delavigne, rule out a connection. The crime bore the stamp of the London murders he had studied. There was, of course, a difference in the choice of location: In London the murderer had attacked his victims in the vicinity of obscure taverns, with which the "Golden Bell" could not be compared. Such a change of milieu went against the rule, unless one assumed that in the strange city the man had misjudged the place. To be sure, there was a theory which had much in its favor: that the murderer was not a seaman, as was popularly assumed, but a physician. The passenger lists were on their way from Dover.

The Inspector had not allowed himself a minute's sleep. After taking leave of Etienne at the Obelisk, he had returned home and at the front door run into the messenger who summoned him to the scene of the crime. He had managed to find a cab and had gone first to his office to pick up the bag containing the equipment that was indispensible to him on such occasions. When he arrived at the "Golden Bell," about three hours had elapsed since the moment the mortal scream had been heard.

According to Delavigne, the Inspector was extremely dissatisfied with what had happened in the meantime. He had relieved his colleague Surdent, who was in charge of the precinct. Murder had priority over every other offense. Busybodies had pushed their way in and destroyed evidence. A number of guests had managed to slip away without being identified. Others had been allowed to leave after Surdent had interrogated them superficially. How could he have let that couple go in front of whose love nest the murder had been committed? That was worse than a blunder.

The confusion had revealed plainly that Surdent, as Dobrowsky put it, "had never had the honor of dealing with murderers." He was a stout, good-natured fellow who was fond of his breakfast. They had transferred him to this quiet precinct behind the Madeleine after he had for years guarded railway stations whenever princes or ministers were welcomed. He knew and admired them all, from Chulalongkorn to the Prince of Wales. He would still go rigid with awe when someone produced a senator's calling card or a diplomat's pass as the little Prussian had done. It was even lucky that Surdent had taken down the address.

Dobrowsky's arrival put an end to the disorder. Though he scarcely moved, the Inspector seemed to be everywhere at once. He gave the order to commence with the medical examination of the corpse and the systematic investigation of the house. He had a special system, which entailed dividing the space into small squares. The doors were locked and guarded, personnel and guests sent to different rooms, some alone, others in groups. In the latter case an undercover man mingled with the guests, not only to observe them, but to loosen their tongues through special tricks.

All this proceeded along the lines of a maneuver—with the routine of fishermen who draw in their net and sort their catch. After Dobrowsky had deployed his men and carefully examined the corridor, he went downstairs to the restaurant. There he had the folding screens that served as partitions removed and a table set up in the middle for himself and the clerks. The lighting had been intensified with glaring lamps that were part of the equipment. The light also fell on the corpse, which was lying on an adjacent table. The coroner had already recorded his initial findings. Moreover, Doctor Besançon was in the house attending to Madame Stephanie. "This is no ordinary crisis—it's the bamboo stroke." The Doctor had served in Indochina. Thus the Inspector was deprived of his most important witness. She alone knew the names of the guests who were particularly careful that their visit left no trace.

Dobrowsky soon had his first results. The dead woman's name was Liane della Rosa—at least that was her stage name, under which she had appeared that very evening. She had been performing for some weeks at the Olympia Theatre, a music hall on the Boulevard des Capucines. The program that was put on there every evening consisted of three parts: a selection of variety numbers, the modern ballet in the middle, and an operetta at the end. Liane performed as soloist in the ballet. With her magnificent body she created a furor as a ballerina; unfortunately she had no singing voice. That is why she usually left the theater at the beginning of the second intermission, at about ten o'clock. Shortly before eleven Bourdin had opened the door to her and her companion.

Up to now there was still no trace of this companion. The Inspector had meanwhile obtained information about the dancer's habits: Liane della Rosa was twenty years old, a sanguine creature, well liked by everybody. Her colleagues and Lagoanère, the director, had only good things to say about her. She appeared frequently in the "Golden Bell"; her company varied. The strange thing was that middle-aged men were missing: she was seen either with very young men or with rather elderly ones—she made a sharp distinction between her heart and her judgment. It had to be one or the other, but not both at the same time.

But someone must have caught a glimpse of the companion, at least when he entered the house. Perhaps he was even known there. Dobrowsky had Bourdin come downstairs—and Madame Stephanie as well, despite the protests of the Doctor, who had revived her for the moment with strong coffee and smelling salts.

Madame Stephanie appeared, propped up on Mademoiselle Picard's good arm. Her ivorylike complexion had taken on a livid pallor; at the sight of the brutal changes in the room she heaved a sigh like a captain who sees his ship going down. Her business was ruined, and it was not a glorious shipwreck. Through the venetian blinds one could hear the murmuring of a crowd that had gathered outside. The "Golden Bell," which had thrived for many years in snug tranquility, now stood in the glare of floodlights. What had become of decency, the cordon of discreet silence, the reputation of a hostess whose equal, even in this city of exquisite pleasures, was not easy to find?

"At Stephanie's" was a codeword among initiates. She valued discretion and had an unfailing eye for cheap wares. Blatant behavior was hardly conceivable among the stock of regulars that had gathered here over the years. She disliked scenes. Just recently she had turned out a shameless old man, although important guests who had brought him along claimed he was a great poet. All that was for nothing. Now, whenever they said "at Madame Stephanie's," other images, hideous ones, would be evoked. A second of inattention had sufficed.

The Inspector had an armchair brought in for her. He had witnessed many breakdowns. In the lurid glare of an atrocity, the shadows, too, grew deeper; it magnified and coarsened the petty weaknesses and faults that are to be found everywhere. For decades an architect had performed his duties, to his own and everyone else's satisfaction. Now a house collapsed, and it was discovered that he had been an unscrupulous scoundrel. Some were astonished that such a man had been trusted, others had known it all along. And so it was with every gatekeeper, indeed even with priests—one dared not look behind their façade, otherwise it would emerge: not only the individual's infamy, but society's as well. Human beings inhabited it like animals on a reef. They sought the lighting that was favorable to them. A ray of truth could be fatal.

For this reason, even the law had to restrict itself and impose limits on inquiries, as everyone knew who had grown familiar with the material. One could shed only as much light as the specific case demanded. Otherwise there was danger that the truth would spread like wildfire. Revolutions usually begin with actions that one fails to hold in check. That is like carrying fire from the stoves. In every thorough investigation one comes up against the social lie in which everyone shares. To expose it is the responsibility of prophets, not of the court. Dobrowsky realized that here in the "Golden Bell" he was taking hold of a hot iron.

Bourdin was a poor witness, utterly confused. She was used to working in the shadows. Now she stood there with her tousled gray hair like a guilty woman in the dock, like an old soldier who had failed on sentry duty. She was a loyal soul, but she could not be left alone. The Inspector had to drag the facts out of her in bits and pieces as from a well. She had known and admired the dancer. But she could say nothing about her companion, however much Dobrowsky pressed her. She did not know whether he was young or old, tall or short, fat or thin. There was a blank space in her memory as on a bad photograph. This seemed strange despite her obtuseness.

"But the man must have said something."

No, he hadn't opened his mouth. Mademoiselle Liane had ordered everything they needed. She knew the house and its customs; that is why letting them in had only taken a moment. The Inspector controlled his impatience; one had to avoid intimidating the old woman. He said in a friendly tone:

"Still, the man did have a face. And the vestibule is well lit. You must have seen him, and you know very well not just anybody is allowed in. I ask you: try to remember exactly."

Bourdin stuck to her statement: "I didn't see him."

"But my good woman, that's simply impossible."

Finally it came out: The man had pulled his hat down over his eyes and held a handkerchief in front of his face—he must have had a nosebleed.

She had in fact not seen his face. At this explanation Madame Stephanie almost fainted again:

"Miserable wretch! You let a man in who was hiding his face. Were you mad?"

The servant tried humbly to defend herself:

"Madame, you know that Miss Liane only came with fine gentlemen. And his coat was of the best material."

Here the Inspector jumped in. He was suddenly wide-awake like a hunting dog that picks up the scent, and fired off a series of direct questions. What color, what cut, what kind of buttons did the coat have, what shape was the hat? Was it a hat like the ones young men wear or elderly gentlemen? She surely must have seen the hand that held the handkerchief, perhaps with a ring, and the shoes. Were they wet or shiny like those worn by a gentleman getting out of a carriage? Had the dancer mentioned the nosebleed or not?

This did not get him very far. Bourdin was like a piece of fruit being squeezed, but like a fruit without juice. The only thing she knew for sure was that there had been no blood on the handkerchief. She would have seen blood. The Inspector had to make do with that. As interrogator he thought a moderate amount of pressure sufficient. The witnesses should not be tired out; they should be made willing to talk, but not eager.

The interrogation in the "Golden Bell" went on into the early hours, while the hawkers were already crying out the news of the murder. At the same time they continued with the investigation of the house. The guests whom Surdent had let go were summoned to the Palais by policemen or by pneumatic dispatch. The director and the dancer's colleagues as well. Nor did the Inspector forget the coachmen and the florists.

25

Nearly an hour passed before Etienne was filled in on the details by Delavigne. Meanwhile he had looked in on Dobrowsky, who during the breaks in the interrogations was busy giving orders. Etienne was trained from his stint with the hussars to take orders given in rapid succession— right from the saddle. But he had to admit that this, compared to what the Inspector had to accomplish, was child's play. There one had clear-cut goals, while here a network was being strung together. It was amazing the way this sleepwalker seemed to shed his slovenly appearance as he gathered momentum. Above all, he was an expert in the art of delegation: while he sat in his office, others were tracking for him in the city as well as in the files. He reminded Etienne of an animal extending tentacles armed with suckers.

The extraordinary offense within the confines of a large city and its advanced civilization explained the general agitation. The reaction was at once violent and primitive. The murder victim was no longer a woman such as one meets by the thousands in the city, and her murderer not just any man. But then again any women might have been the victim, and every man was now a suspect. People regarded each other with fear and suspicion. The blaze had to be extinguished before it spread. Dobrowsky knew his responsibility.

Etienne went across to his office; Delavigne accompanied him. In the hallway messengers were carrying bundles of posters right off the press like stacks of red linen. Etienne was seized by the vague notion that he was in a theater lobby. With such comparisons he had already compromised himself in Nancy.

In its disorder, Dobrowsky's office resembled a command post during battle. Along the walls stood shelves full of green cartons and volumes of official bulletins. On the large table in the center were piles of dossiers, papers, and telegrams. The Inspector was seated behind it with his assistants; he was taking a break between the interrogations. The ashtrays had been emptied and fresh coffee served. There was a coming and going as in a marketplace.

Dobrowsky was busy rolling a supply of cigarettes. He greeted his friend. Then he spread out one of the posters that had been brought in: MURDER in foot-long letters—a blood-red shimmer passed over his face, giving it the sated rigidity of a Mexican god. He was content; the Minister was offering a large reward. Such a case was always welcome to the authorities; it confirmed their indispensibility and occupied the masses. One had—almost like when the Prussians came—a common enemy.

The Inspector gave the sheet to Delavigne and pointed to

a batch of telegrams: "Still getting passenger lists from the Channel steamers."

"You're thoroughly convinced, then, that he's come over from London?"

Dobrowsky shrugged his shoulders to Etienne's question: "We must proceed according to the rules of the profession: that is essential to controlling the bottlenecks." Etienne recalled that the Inspector had once explained this rule to him: When a large city is divided by a river, then during the search for a suspect the bridges become the bottleneck which it is crucial to occupy. That belongs to the economy of the manhunt. In this case it was the Channel that served as bottleneck. If the monster had come over from London, then it was likely that his name was on one of the lists. Place and time were given; the rest was a matter of detail.

"But he will have traveled under an assumed name." The trainee had raised this objection. The Inspector nodded to him: "Delavigne, I thank you for this suggestion. If the man is as intelligent as you think, it won't be long till we've caught him. There is nothing more conspicuous than assuming a false name—you stand out among hundreds of names in the records as Mister Unknown. And the stewards have an enviable memory.

Dobrowsky had once said to Etienne: "Our friend Delavigne would make a poor criminal—that says something for him as a person, but not as a police trainee."

Apropos bottlenecks, he had told Etienne on one of their walks about a case he had managed to solve some years before. Near the Swiss border they had found a tourist beside a mountain path who evidently had been the victim of murder and robbery. The corpse was lying close by a summit that was frequented by crowds of excursionists. Who could have been the murderer? Probably a beginner, some anonymous person among the millions of a large city who was up to his neck in trouble and had set out to waylay, kill, and rob the first one to come along. Crimes like these are difficult to investigate because they are committed by people without imagination. The more subtly one goes about it, the more snares he puts in his own path.

Nevertheless, the Inspector succeeded in his search, and in the following way: Whoever scaled that mountain usually spent the night at its foot, either on the Swiss or on the French side; there were two spas there. The bullet found at the autopsy had been fired from a Belgian pistol which was often sold in France. For that reason, the Inspector began the inquiry on the French side by sifting the guestbooks of the hotels and boarding houses. The inn-keepers could provide information about a good many of the names obtained in this way; those in question were visitors who were more or less known to them. They could be disregarded for the time being; it was unlikely that the perpetrator was to be found among them. The remaining names were verified after inquiries at the places of residence. Following this routine one comes across people time and again who have registered under a false name; almost without exception men who were not spending the night by themselves. These, too, could be eliminated, for it was a sure bet that the murderer had come alone.

In the course of this meticulous work, the Inspector came across a curious entry. It led to a real and yet non-existent person, a dead man who could not possibly have entered his name himself, although he was there in the registers. He was identified as a resident of Lyon who had been lying buried for the last three years in a local cemetery.

The rest was simple: the Inspector had examined the dead man's circle of acquaintances very closely and had soon found the perpetrator: a petty tradesman who was being pressured by his creditors, a person utterly lacking in imagination.

"You see—the only bit of intelligence he showed cost him his head. The idea that nobody is more undiscoverable than a dead man wasn't bad, but there was a short circuit. When I interrogated him I could summon two ghosts as witnesses against him: his victim and his dead friend. I've seldom seen such devastation."

Dobrowsky was an excellent theoretician. He could have written a manual for police officers, as Clausewitz had for soldiers or Dufresne for chess players. Etienne had told him that yesterday. He recalled the conversation in which Delavigne had been advised of the disadvantages of ano-nymity. The latter was insistent:

"If anyone can catch the man with the handkerchief, chief, it's you and no one else."

"Thank you for your confidence. But the man with the

handkerchief will soon come of his own accord, like all the others who were in the "Golden Bell"—with one exception. Such a murder is like a floodlight. The moths draw near the glare."

"So you're saying he wasn't the one who did it?"

"There's nobody more harmless."

Etienne, too, was surprised. He had shared Delavigne's opinion. It was also Madame Stephanie's. But the Inspector's hypothesis was convincing:

The unfortunate dancer had clearly been in a hurry the evening before. She had disappeared after the director had detained her and turned up with a companion a short time later in the vestibule of the "Golden Bell." The time was established—it was just enough to cover the distance between the theater and the Madeleine in a cab—they were looking for the driver; perhaps he had already been found. So della Rosa must have had a rendezvous; after all, she was not one to let herself be solicited on the street. Her impatience suggested further that she had arranged to meet one of her young admirers, perhaps for the first time—a novice whom one did not like to keep waiting. An older man is made to dance attendance and is gotten rid of as soon as possible.

Here the Inspector, though time was short, could not refrain from a digression: "I will admit that della Rosa hasn't the stature of the beautiful Otéro, who is also said to have once honored the "Golden Bell" with her presence. They say that before dinner she lifts her soup plate and starts bleeding from the nose if she doesn't find a thousand franc bill underneath. She gets up and is never seen again."

He took up the thread again: "The nosebleed is a sign of embarrassment—it might be construed as an intensified blush. That immediately rules out the man with the handkerchief as the murderer. A person with such a terrible design doesn't appear in the light, and certainly not with his face covered—that is, with a gesture that announces at first glance: there is something wrong here. He must have come alone and in the dark."

Dobrowsky had more coffee brought in and concluded his observations. Unshaven and bleary-eyed, at the same time as vigorous as a doped racehorse, he seemed even more disheveled than usual. Etienne thought: "Somewhere in Poland among his ancestors there must have been a shrewd rabbi." It was more than a vision.

No—behind the handkerchief had been one of Liane's boys; it was probably his first excursion into this realm. One of those who sent notes and flowers to the ballerina's dressing room or attempted to catch her eye when she left the theater. He had been intimidated by Bourdin, and the dancer had found that amusing. A fine young fellow; student at a military academy or an expensive boarding school. Many were already customers of the best tailors; it was altogether incredible how much money they had. He was now lying somewhere in Saint-Cyr or Neuilly, had reported sick and pulled the blanket up over his head, out of his mind with fear. Soon he would not be able to take it any longer.

That sounded plausible, indeed obvious. As if to corroborate it, a policeman came in and announced Gerhard zum Busche.

26

After Surdent had read his card and respectfully dismissed him, Gerhard had wandered about aimlessly in the fog. He had answered the inspector as in a dream. From that moment he was utterly confused, having lost his bearings in time and space.

His condition confirmed his aunt's fears. First he had followed the bank of the river and then ended up in the woods without knowing how he had gotten there. As it began to get light, he found himself at the edge of a pond, and before him loomed a cliff. It was the houses of Suresnes.

He drifted about like a castaway. A wave had destroyed his boat. The wave was rosy as it ascended and black on the other side. The guilt was so intense that it cast a pall over the events of the night before—they were all jumbled together; he confused them. Why had he brought Irene to that house? He had murdered her there—why had he sent her the roses?

It was very hot. In the abyss human beings were not distinct; they melted into each other like tin figures. Now he was the murderer, now he wasn't—however much he turned the guilt over in his mind, he was not assuaged. And even if Irene had only seemingly been the murder victim, and the murder victim only seemingly Irene—it remained an agonizing, inextricable entanglement. Had he not taken her there, none of this would have happened. He had touched the forbidden door. Irene was another man's wife. He had sent her roses. Now his hand was stained with blood.

Then his thoughts strayed in another direction. Instead of revering this image, he had dragged it down from its sphere, he had desired it. He had listened to Ducasse. The murder had been planned, what had happened in front of the door was no accident. The judgment was that compelling.

Gradually his will returned. There was no explaining away his guilt; he would have to answer for it. But Irene was in danger. He had to protect her, shield her from the disastrous consequences.

When he entered his apartment, a policeman was waiting for him with Dobrowsky's summons. The officer accompanied him to the Palais de Justice and announced his arrival.

The Inspector said: "The Polonaise begins." He considered the young diplomat his most valuable witness, except for the man with the handkerchief. As Gerhard was led in, Dobrowsky saw immediately whom he was dealing with. Obviously he, too, had had his first adventure in the "Golden Bell." Instead of fulfillment, it had given him a shock for the rest of his life.

The young man was pale and distraught—a Raskolnikov figure? After taking one look at him, the Inspector dismissed this idea. Thanks to long experience this sort of stupor was familiar to him. Here it seemed unusually powerful. It was conceivable that this young man—he looked almost like a child—had been moving about in an imaginary world. Then he had fallen from a twofold height. In any case, he would have to be handled gently, otherwise his poor mind would take leave of him forever. In that sense it was good that Surdent had not interrogated him. These people often cause more damage when they are zealous than when they loaf.

He pushed a chair over to Gerhard, offered him coffee and cigarettes. Gerhard was grateful for the coffee; it was wonderfully invigorating. Here, at least, he felt more comfortable than in the woods. He had expected to be received by a committee of stern faces, but the man who had offered him the coffee looked more like a clerk; he seemed to be friendly.

While Gerhard was drinking, the Inspector reassured him with the usual commonplaces. He regretted that they had to meet under such terrible circumstances. He would ask some questions later; that might clear up the fait accompli which had taken Gerhard so brutally by surprise. Then he could go home and get some rest. The Inspector avoided using the word "murder."

"Perhaps you would rather talk in private. But if you have no objection my colleague will join us. He could be of some help to us."

He pointed to Etienne, with whom Gerhard had already exchanged a glance.

"I would like that, Inspector—the gentleman has a good face. He doesn't look like a policeman."

Dobrowsky laughed: "That's what I call candor. There's no need to worry that you'll withhold much information."

He rose and led them both into his private office. It was more like a dressing room, a bare space with little furniture: a table, a clothesstand and a sink. There was an ashtray on the table, but no writing implement. A closet was scarcely noticeable, since the doors were covered with matching wallpaper. A larger than life-size mirror between the windows had a curious effect. On either side of its frame a scale was marked in centimeters. The numbers were joined by fine lines which had apparently been scratched in the glass with a diamond.

Etienne knew the room, which, as noted, gave the impression of a cloakroom that one enters but for a moment. In fact, that is what it was. The Inspector disposed of his hat, umbrella, and coat here before he went on duty. He also came here at times to wash his hands or meditate while smoking a cigarette at the window when he needed to take a break. It was common knowledge that on certain evenings he left his cabinet in disguise. That was the point of the mirror and the contents of the closet, which bore resemblance to a junk shop. The room had double doors; but that an interrogation was held here was an exception.

27

After they had sat down, there was a long silence. The Inspector seemed to reflect; his expression gradually intensified, his eyes grew shiny, the wrinkles taut. It was as if a drug were beginning to take effect or the skin were being massaged by an invisible hand. Etienne was familiar with this strain. He was astonished to see it in the presence of a witness who seemed so insignificant and probably had even less to say than Bourdin. Of course, he had been the first to see the corpse.

After a long while Dobrowsky turned to Gerhard and laid a hand on his arm:

"You lost your father at an early age, Herr zum Busche, but you should trust me now as if you were sitting across from him—that will do you good. Nothing human is foreign to me."

"I'll be glad to tell you everything," Gerhard replied and then added: "As far as it concerns me."

It did not surprise him that this man seemed to know his family. Perhaps he knew how to read faces the way others did books; this had to be a man of knowledge. Naturally the Inspector had obtained information from the police's political section as well as from the Rue de Lille. The dossiers on foreign delegations and their personnel, right down to the cleaning women, were being maintained at the moment with particular thoroughness. He was already informed, at least with the main points, about most of the guests of the evening before. "An absolute mess," he had murmured upon reading Surdent's list.

Gerhard's qualification did not come as a surprise to him—he already knew where the boy's shoe was pinching.

Gerhard could not know that he was no exception—on the contrary. Two of the guests had already appeared in person, others had sent short notes. The Prefect had called up and requested that a senator be treated discreetly. One had to be several places at once.

He said:

"I can reassure you—divulging names is not in the interests of the police. We'll see what can be done. I trust your statement will suffice."

Gerhard felt increasingly at ease; the room seemed more hospitable. He could withhold Irene's name after all—it was almost like being examined by a careful physician; the tender spot would not be touched.

The Inspector now took a map out of his briefcase and spread it out on the table. It showed the ground plan of the first floor of the "Golden Bell" with notes and measurements. He lined up a little ruler and a compass.

"Please point to where you were standing when the crime took place."

After Gerhard had pointed to the door, Dobrowsky asked:

"Did you notice anything before you heard the scream? Sounds, footsteps in the corridor, or someone knocking?"

Yes, the shadowy face that had appeared right before behind the pane of frosted glass. The Inspector gave a start as if he, too, were terrified. That was something new: evidence that was missing in Surdent's protocol. He asked Gerhard to stand in front of the mirror and compared the diamond's scratches with the measurements. The witness had seen the entire head.

"It must have been a rather tall man, even if I assume that he was standing on tiptoe."

That the man might have had a beard was something Gerhard would not rule out—but he was certain that he had not worn a hat. The face had appeared in the windowpane as in a frame.

"Strange," said Etienne, "I've always imagined this Jack as being sturdy and broad-shouldered like most seamen, and with a cap on his head."

"I, too. But those are precisely the notions one should not heed."

Dobrowsky now went into detail, repeating the same questions again and again, which kept him busy for almost an hour. The patience with which he was able to stretch the seconds between the appearance of the face and the scream in order to gain new points of departure revealed long years of experience—and no less the adroitness with which he refreshed Gerhard's memory.

He had once said to Etienne: "Our memory retains more than we know—for instance, when we look for a quote whose wording has slipped our mind, we still remember the place where it stood: at the top or at the bottom, on the right or on the left page. A good interrogation takes the opposite path—it first establishes the place and then brings things to light which the witness has forgotten or considered unimportant."

The Inspector seemed already to know more than Etienne had surmised—whether from Surdent's protocol or thanks to his own investigation. Evidently he had also given Bourdin another grilling. He now meticulously went into the subject of the lighting. In this regard Madame Stephanie made arrangements to fit the circumstances. The house was brightly lit when a private party was scheduled, otherwise the corridors were dim. So it had been the previous evening—Gerhard recalled that Bourdin had escorted him upstairs with a lamp.

When a door opened, someone leaving the room could hardly be recognized from the corridor, or only in silhouette. On the other hand, what went on outside the room could be seen more distinctly from inside, since the brighter light fell upon the corridor. The ghastly sight of the murdered woman had made an indelible impression on Gerhard.

Moreover, he had only seen the face behind the glass because light from the room had fallen on it. The Inspector asked once again whether it was bearded. That was possible, but the frosted glass had blurred the contours—as though ink had spilled onto a blotter, and it only lasted a moment.

"So when you unbolted the door after hearing the scream, the corridor was dark, or only half dark, except for the beam of light coming from your room."

Returning to the noises. The corridors in the "Golden Bell" were covered with thick carpets, so the witness could scarcely have heard footsteps, or only muffled ones. But in front of the adjoining room, shortly after the face had disappeared and before the scream had rung out, something must have happened. Had Gerhard heard the door being opened or someone knocking at it? Voices, perhaps? Whispering or laughter? There were different kinds—

depending on whether one sees an acquaintance, a stranger, a mask.

That was hard to answer. Between the face and the scream Gerhard had heard only a murmur, although he had listened anxiously. But then he recalled the voice that had cried out: "Let go of me!"

Strange that he had forgotten it; the scream must have blotted it out.

That was the second surprise for the Inspector; he broke off the interrogation for a while. After he had smoked a cigarette at the window, he asked: "So you heard the dancer's last word, a cry of terror—do you remember it exactly? For example: there is hardly a difference between 'laissez' and 'laisse.'"

No: "laissez"—there Gerhard was certain.

Then back to the adjoining door. It was also possible that it had been open. This was highly unlikely, for in this case the intrusion of a stranger would have been followed by an exchange of words and surely some noise as well. Nothing of the kind had been heard. Here the suspicion cast upon the dancer's companion was compelling—but wouldn't the man with the handkerchief have had it easier inside than in the corridor? Of course, he could have pursued her there. Her cry of terror seemed rather to suggest a stranger. But one could not afford to exclude any possibility. Sometimes the wrong paths led to success. The interrogation seemed to be over; the Inspector sighed:

"Thank you, Herr zum Busche. You can go now."

And then, as if something else occurred to him:

"Madame de Kargané will probably have little to add to that. Unfortunately, she suddenly left on a trip last night."

Etienne saw Gerhard go pale at this sudden attack, then blush. The Inspector had pulled the rug out from under him; the house of cards collapsed in which he had felt so secure. Etienne now understood why his friend had not conducted the examination in proper sequence, beginning not with the vestibule, but right off with what had happened on the second floor. So that had not been maladroitness—on the contrary. Now he struck home; he became aggressive:

"Are you really so simple-minded that you didn't stop to think what sort of establishment you were being asked to come to? And about the fact that your lady friend was known there, though not by her real name? But she not only left her hat on the mantelpiece, she also forgot her cape and in it your note. The hat alone would have sufficed."

Dobrowsky then addressed the matter of the dispute that had taken place when they came in; the servant woman had already made her statement. No doubt, the Countess had resented being greeted as a customer. It had been particularly galling for Bourdin to have the word "tramp" thrown in her face. After all, she really had meant well. But why—that she had not disclosed, and the Inspector now heard from Gerhard: she had apologized to Madame de Kargané for *her* room being already taken.

That was the third surprise for Dobrowsky; it was the quote he had been looking for without knowing the words.

The Inspector would spend his midday break relaxing on the nearby quay, watching the fishermen. They seemed to be sitting there more to pass the time, reeling in only an occasional gudgeon. Then they would put it in a small bucket and cast their lines again, waiting until the float twitched, a piece of cork with a feather that was dyed red at the tip. When they hauled in the line, usually only the bait had been nibbled away—but that at least showed that there were fish around.

A similar twitch came over the Inspector at this point in the interrogation. Why had Bourdin recalled the "tramp," but concealed the reason she had been abused? Dobrowsky was acquainted with the dim light of receptions, from the ordinary right up to the luxurious establishments. That was a chapter in itself, and this included the little tricks by which the personnel bettered their wages. When a room was not hired for the night, but only for an hour, it could happen that the porter, or in this case Bourdin, pocketed the money and omitted the entry from the list of guests. That explained her stubborn reticence on this point. She may have been simple-minded, but when the sous was at stake she was quite cunning. Thus she had seized the opportunity when the reception, which Madame Stephanie usually attended to herself, had been put in her charge. That is why she had asked the Countess immediately how long she was planning to stay. That she could give her, instead of "her" room, only the adjoining one helped camouflage the ruse. Thus a gap was put to use.

Certainly, it was a minor matter; nonetheless, like the

twitching of the float, it signaled movement in murky water. The Inspector turned to Gerhard: "Herr zum Busche, you can go home now. You should get a good night's sleep. Tomorrow things will look different; time will cool things off. You can count on our discretion."

28

When he was alone with Etienne, the Inspector took the guest list of the "Golden Bell" out of his briefcase and placed a small, leather-bound engagement book next to it on the table. Etienne said:

"My compliments—but don't you think you treated him a bit underhandedly? I feel sorry for him."

"Believe me, Etienne—it bothers me, too. But the boy is like a mimosa—if I had come down hard on him at the very beginning, I wouldn't have gotten a word out of him. As it was, I guided him like a sleepwalker." He added:

"Besides, I reassured him against my better judgment. Think of the press; there have been crowds of reporters at the doors since early morning. And the cuckolded husband? An extremely dangerous character. No doubt his name will be in all the evening papers, no matter what we do. I don't know how this dreamer is going to get through it all, indeed, whether he'll survive it."

The fog had lifted completely. The sun over the river was casting reflections through the window that rippled along the ceiling. Dobrowsky seemed tired and drifted off into general observations. He returned to the subject of the press.

A policeman has a different stake in a crime than a journalist, since he represents the State rather than society. There are crimes which affect not only the victim and the perpetrator, but also to a large extent the social milieu, for example, the gruesome murder of his wife by the Duke de Praslin. They had smuggled him some poison, but too late, which had given the impression of complicity: birds of a feather. A peer of France had murdered like a drunken servant and thought of himself as something better. The monarchy had never recovered from this shock.

And then the crimes that became fashionable, including suicides. Someone would burn himself alive in the woods or jump off a high bridge, others would copy him. Timon, not exactly a philanthropist, at a public gathering: "Athenians—several people have already hanged themselves from my fig tree. I have to cut it down. So whoever wants to hang himself had better hurry!"

Worth noting were cases in which the series was used as camouflage. A teller whose bank had been robbed twice simulated a third break-in in order to enrich himself; these were conjuring tricks.

Etienne was familiar with these digressions. He knew that beneath the surface his friend was pursuing his combinations as under a loosely woven fabric. Once again he took up the subject of the "Golden Bell."

"I find it more and more unlikely that this was the doing

of someone who works *behind* the mast. It's not his milieu—much rather that of the man with the handkerchief. But I'm ruling him out. That's what my instinct tells me; still, I must follow up every lead. After all, he is the key figure. If he forgot to bolt the door, then surely the dancer didn't. How do you explain that nobody knocked and that no sound was heard at all until right before the scream? Where could he have gone? Was he hiding—then he was caught in a trap; at the latest, Surdent would have found him. So it can be assumed that he fled. But then he would have been seen; the corridor was bustling at that point. It could be that he had mingled with the other guests. In Surdent's list there is no indication of this. Whatever the case—his disappearance remains a mystery."

"Then he could have been the one after all?"

"That would be the simplest solution. Then we wouldn't have to be bothered with a second disappearance: that of the murderer himself. I'm not willing to accept this. But I can't rule it out. Like it or not, we have to deal with the dancer's friends. That would scatter us like hare and hounds. I've delegated it to the *police des moeurs*, can't do everything myself, after all. They're fine trackers, at least on this trail; here's the first report already."

He pointed to the guest list of the "Golden Bell"; some places he had marked with a red pencil. Gerhard's visit, in fact, had not been entered, but that of the dancer in number Twelve had, in almost illegible handwriting. The other entries were of little help either—for example, "Philippe Onze et Épouse." Hardly anyone had entered his real name, except perhaps some actors like the one Madame de Kargané had once arrived with. The guestbook was more a reflector of morals than a document. But the police looked the other way.

Better results were obtained from the dancer's notebook, which she had purchased at the beginning of the year at Hautecoeur's fine leather department—a tiny date book with a list of addresses that had been found in her handbag. One of Bertillon's novices had examined it. The Inspector commented: "The girl had a sense of order—I must say."

Beneath the dates were notes concerning the theater: try-outs, rehearsals, performances. The list of addresses served at the same time as a record of the gifts she had received. They had amounted to several times her pay.

"Those were her old men," said Dobrowsky, "we'll track them down. It seems that for her old age already began at forty; but the young ones could not be much over twenty. They're missing in her engagement book; apparently she needed no reminders for these rendezvous."

Just under the fateful date there was an exception: "11 P.M. Le Bleu." That might be a nickname. Perhaps it referred to the eyes, or the suit—a uniform?

In any case, the colleague had done his work well. He had also discovered that certain numbers were filled in with ink like the heads of musical notes.

"Take a look at this three. It's a Sunday; the upper loop has been inked in. And here the nine, an ordinary day with a red cap—on both days no rendezvous."

Dobrowsky shoved the notebook aside: "It's a shame

about this person. She would have gone far in life. Madame Stephanie was especially fond of her."

That was true; surely it was due less to chance than to an affinity shared by temperaments who knew how to make the most of their talents. Once she had recovered from the shock, they would be able to get quite a lot out of Madame Stephanie. She had a good memory, and when she saw the charming hat that the Countess had lost while fleeing, she immediately remembered the lady who had already been there with the young actor in number Twelve. In this she concurred with Bourdin. Most hotels do not have a "Thirteen"—the adjoining room, "Fourteen," had nevertheless turned out to be disastrous.

Herr zum Busche evidently thought that he had been there with a princess. That is an optical illusion which most young men succumb to on their first adventure, and that was doubtless the case here.

"I didn't dare tell him the whole truth—he's incredibly naive."

There is a Hippocratic face in the moral sphere as well. The Inspector had an eye for it; his profession had sharpened his vision. He said: "I feel rather uneasy about him."

29

Like many criminologists, Dobrowsky had studied the tactics of the London criminal even before the incident in

ERNST JÜNGER

the "Golden Bell." It was the case of a century. Even a theater had already profited from it.

The Paris murder deviated considerably from what is known in jargon as the "dodge"—especially in the underworld. The Londoner had always escaped because he had moved on level ground. Was it conceivable that he had ventured onto the second floor as into a mousetrap? The back door was hard to find and, except for this single day, securely locked—everything seemed to point to someone who knew his way around here.

What if it had been someone who was out to settle a score and deliberately copied the terrible Jack's trademark—a case of mimicry? Perhaps to damage the hostess in the most severe way possible? The dancer was just the first to cross his path.

Etienne shook his head: "Inspector—here you're like a billiard player trying to bank a shot off an impossible cushion."

Dobrowsky countered: "With human beings nothing is impossible. We have to examine everyone who knew the back entrance, including the deliverymen. We're caught in a tangle of facts, a veritable jungle—I'd like to see the elephant's trunk."

Delavigne's return interrupted the conversation. He had been in the morgue, where the corpse had been taken after the autopsy. Before that there had been a dispute among the doctors about the instrument with which the murder had been committed. It could only have been a knife—a very sharp one, but every trade uses one or even several like that.

Della Rosa had been scantily dressed when she opened the door. The contrast between the wonderful body and the horrifying wound had shocked the assistant. "To think that there are people who still believe in God."

Dobrowsky asked several more questions, then said: "Delavigne—you can prove yourself—I have some work for you."

The assistant was first to have a look at what was going on at the Karganés, but avoid meeting the Captain in case he was at home. Inquiries: First, learn from the footman, who had gone in and out the day before; second, from the coachman, if he had made any trips and where; third, from the chambermaid, what perfumes the Countess had used.

"Go from there to Guerlain—another perfumery is out of the question—and ask for a copy of the list of clients the salesmen take along on their rounds."

Finally, the assistant was to call on Monsieur Ducasse. Delavigne asked while taking down some notes: "What's doing there?"

"Engage him in a conversation to find out something about Monsieur zum Busche—he had lunch with him yesterday at Voisin. At the same time Madame de Kargané was seen with her father at one of the tables. It seems it was there that the *coup de foudre* between her and this idiot took place. Here's the address—don't let them put you off. He will probably answer the door himself. And come back soon; I still have plenty for you to do."

Delavigne left; Etienne accompanied him. He had almost forgotten that he had an engagement with Du Paty—luckily right nearby in the "Tour d'Argent." He was going to bore him again with the Master of Bayreuth, whom he revered—partly out of conviction, partly because it was the fashion.

"Inspector, I'll make it short. I'll be back here in two hours."

After leaving the Palais, he descended to the walled-in tip of the island, the Square du Vert Galand. The sun shone on the buildings along the banks, on the bridges and the river. On the lawn children were playing, watched by their mothers or nursery maids. A large riverboat was anchored at the quay, connected to it by a narrow gangplank. Smoke swirled from its funnel, laundry was hung out on the deck. That was surely a fine profession—one was always traveling and always at home like a snail in its shell. At the great registration of the world they must have forgotten these boatsmen; they lived as in former times. Perhaps their children didn't need to go to school.

The train of a weeping willow trailed in the gray stream. It was already sprinkled with yellow strands. Trees are better off than humans, who turn gray in autumn—they turn bright.

Where the willow touched the water it merged with its mirror image: with a second willow which was darker. Image and mirror image almost seemed reversed—the willow in the water was more real. In the shadow of the tree stood Gerhard zum Busche—he must have been lingering there for some time. Etienne thought: he's standing there like someone reciting a poem. He wondered whether he should approach him, but decided against it—it was probably better that way. He wanted to spare him further torment.

PART THREE

30

Gerhard did not know how long he had been standing at the edge of the river staring into the water. Finally he decided to go back to his apartment; he went on foot to the Rue Bellechasse. In front of the house entrance stood a charabanc like those used for country excursions.

Madame Lipp, his landlady, was waiting for him in the vestibule: "My God! Just where have you been? Your aunt has asked for you twice already. But you look ill—I'm going to call a doctor."

"Under no circumstances. I only need some rest."

Of course—he had not been home all night, which had never happened before. Madame Lipp did not know whether she was coming or going—an impudent journalist had rung the bell and pestered her with questions at the door, "then the gentleman came who is waiting inside—he wouldn't be put off."

When she had finally opened the door to his room, Gerhard saw a stranger standing at the window. He was in a hunting costume with a wide belt and was holding a crop in his hand. After he had looked Gerhard over attentively, he nodded and said:

"Kargané."

That struck home like a blow to the chest. It was the tribunal.

"Your wife is innocent!"

The Captain raised his hand: "I know, I know. But that's not the point. Why don't we sit down."

This sounded almost conciliatory. And after scrutinizing Gerhard again like someone taking a measurement:

"I've seen you once before, briefly. You have a face one forgets, but that one recognizes. It corresponds exactly to my wife's fantasies. She has good taste, but not a lucky hand."

Madame Lipp came in and asked if they would like a refreshment; the Captain declined.

"I didn't want to spoil her little outing and went hunting in Rambouillet—a fine terrain. Was supposed to meet someone there anyway. When I returned, the police were in the house—I haven't even had time to change, can only stay for a short while, I'm afraid."

He rose to his feet: "Madame Kargané is at her father's; the troublesome incident was unforeseeable. I can imagine how it ruined her mood. And my hunting party—three hours in the shooting stand without seeing so much as a shadow—a devil of a night."

It seemed to Gerhard as if the Captain filled up the room like the main character on a stage, where he was performing a role that he, Gerhard, did not understand. As a child he had had similar feelings toward adults. He stood on the periphery as a nameless being for whom their actions were strange—they astonished and disquieted him. A fatherless child, an orphan.

The powerful man was dominating the stage; what had

happened during the night was becoming shadowy, almost like a dream. Even the guilt was fading; but that was less a deliverance than a further annihilation in his sense of self. The role into which he had been drawn exceeded his capacities; he was not fit for it.

The Captain tapped Gerhard's shoulder with his crop; his voice sounded benevolent.

"This Ducasse is a twaddling scandalmonger; that's no company for you. Now he's rubbing his hands, but in Paris one forgets quickly. In a month the whole thing will have blown over."

Kargané bowed and took his leave; his visit had only lasted a few minutes. Was that to be taken as the end—the resolving of a scandal by denying its significance? One shut himself up at home or went on a trip and let the storm pass. One disregarded the judgment of society. Then, without the involvement in a crime, one might say that next to nothing had happened. Such things went on here night after night, like a swarm of mayflies over the Seine.

These were not questions Gerhard put to himself, yet they were in keeping with his mood; even pain and terror were more real than an empty, senseless world. Madame Lipp, who had escorted the Captain downstairs, now returned and roused him from his brooding:

"What a day. Another gentleman insisting I show him in—even if you were in bed. Have you ever heard of such a thing?"

She handed Gerhard a card, not forgetting, in spite of everything, to present it to him on a tray:

GUY DE MAUCLERC
Authorized Agent Of Count Kargané

Right behind the landlady the visitor entered the room. He must have been waiting downstairs in the carriage, for he was in a hunting coat like the Captain.

Gerhard was unable to get up. He gestured to the place where Kargané had been sitting, but the visitor remained standing.

"Attaché—pardon my inappropriate attire, but I am here on a mission that allows no delay. Count Kargané was offended by you—indeed, as grievously as a man can possibly be offended. He expects satisfaction. I ask you as his second whether you accept the challenge?"

A silence ensued. At last Gerhard said: "The Countess is innocent."

"That is not at issue here. In that case your conduct would only be all the more unpardonable. I am simply to ask you whether you are ready to answer for it with weapons."

And when Gerhard did not answer: "Herr zum Busche—I understand your consternation. As I assume you know what is required among gentlemen, I take your consent for granted. The matter suffers no delay; Count Kargané would like to have it settled early tomorrow morning and then, should he be able, leave on a trip—you understand that he is loath to remain in the city."

And as Gerhard still said nothing: "I see you are ailing—but you will not report sick. It will suffice if you give me the name of your second—I will make the necessary arrangements with him. You needn't worry about a thing—just be on the spot tomorrow."

Mauclerc rightly assumed that the young diplomat was acquainted with the formalities. After an affront such as this, satisfaction was imperative, in fact inevitable. Gerhard was a peaceable dreamer; pleasure in weapons was alien to him. But that he was familiar with the rules of his class from childhood and that he accepted them unquestioningly went without saying. He was also aware of his guilt. Perhaps in this way it could be somewhat diminished.

He had no friends in the city. Among the many acquaintances he had made in the course of his work, only a few—since he preferred to live with imaginary figures—had left an impression on his memory. Hearing Mauclerc impatiently repeat his question about a second, he let them pass in mental review—finally he remembered the Rittmeister.

Mauclerc, who was more and more inclined to think that he was dealing with an idiot, hastily took his leave after writing down the address. The Rittmeister lived in the neighborhood; he knew him by name.

31

Wilhelm von Goldhammer had not yet gotten out of bed, although the afternoon sunlight was already slanting through the curtains. The air in the room was close, hardly a sound came from outside. It was an apartment in the house on the corner of the Rue de Regard and Rue du Cherche-Midi. The location was hardly appropriate to his rank. Schwartzkoppen, his chief, had pointed this out to him; he found it unsuitable for security reasons as well. But Goldhammer loved the ambience with its shabby houses and the petits bourgeois who inhabited them. He did not really know what they did; surely most of them were employed, others lived on small pensions, still others were inscrutable—that suited him just fine. Many had dogs they took for walks in the evening, there were plenty of cats, too. One did not see any whores; the nearest had installed themselves in the vicinity of the Gare Montparnasse. An elegant carriage would occasionally pull up among the scrawny teams of the peddlars—belonging no doubt to a customer of the antique shops, strangely luxurious enclaves in this rather dismal quarter. A side street led to modest studios of painters and sculptors. There could also be unusual scenes where the street intersects the Boulevard Raspail: in front of the military prison—especially when an important prisoner was awaiting his sentence there. Gold-hammer knew this anachronistic bastille; he had already been there in the course of his duties.

There were also green islands amidst these old walls: the gardens of abandoned monasteries, of course only visible from a bird's-eye view. All this seemed at first glance to be simple, but was in fact many-faceted—busy and lethargic, but also conflict-ridden. The concierges could tell many a story that would have appealed to a Balzac.

Goldhammer felt at home here. He, too, was conflict-ridden —one could even say: made up of a whole series of individuals. It can happen that one furthers the other; we then speak not only of a rich, but of a fortunate disposition. With Goldhammer it was rather the opposite. His character, as noted, resembled that of the quarter—there was much pieced together that harmonized poorly, or only in twilight. Among the houses of the Cherche-Midi there was also a dilapidated palace that scarcely stood out from the other buildings—ruin had established equality.

It was only when Goldhammer had drunk heavily, approaching the limit at which consciousness disintegrates, that he sensed an inner harmony. That brought him deliverance, if only for one night; it was also the reason he drank. He had reached the state where his addiction could no longer be concealed. It was interrupted by phases of strict sobriety. Just one year before, in a sanatorium in Wiesbaden, he had held out very well, not touching a glass for months. But then came the young Emperor's birthday—at last another dashing monarch on the throne. He had been sitting in the casino with his wine bottle full of seltzer in front of him—right up to the toast and the anthem: "Goldhammer—a glass of champagne to the Emperor!" There was no refusing. The next day around the same time he was overcome by an irresistable thirst, and soon they were saying again: Goldhammer drinks.

Two of the individuals dwelling in him would have complemented each other well: the Strong and the Just—

Goldhammer was both a good soldier and an astute jurist. Personally he preferred the soldier; that is why, even more than "Doctor," he wished to be called "Herr Rittmeister"—that reminded him of his best days.

He had studied law in Bonn. That had been a rather long interlude before he returned to the army. His dissertation had, of course, been "summa," but only after a bitter dispute among the professors as to whether this intelligent and at the same time unfathomable work should be awarded this grade: "The Concept of Sovereignty in the State and in the Individual." But the argumentation was convincing and so well substantiated by quotes that the decision could be founded on its historical value.

The days when he had been enthusiastic about Hobbes and Stirner were long past. "Who knows what would have become of me if I had had a day laborer for a father—perhaps a burglar or an anarchist. And even then I would be better than the man I am today."

He had always had money, and no doubt too much money. In the administration he had attained the rank of assessor and in the army that of Rittmeister—in other words, neither judge nor staff officer. He had failed to "take the major's hurdle," as they call it. The sudden change in a man's best years is not unknown; on the way to a position of responsibility there is a hitch, either in performance or in character, as here with Goldhammer. There is an increase in the number of embarrassing notes in the personal file—debts, divorce, bad behavior with men and women, neglect of duty. With Goldhammer it was drinking, and that was not all.

He had to admit that time after time they had looked the other way, for he was popular with his superiors as well as with the men. Just as he had different characters, he also had different temperaments—above all (and especially when he had had only a little to drink) that of the born Rhinelander: a contagious gaiety. Thus fatherly admonitions had not been infrequent. "That on more than one occasion you were late or didn't come to work at all is bad enough—but at least during the meeting you should be sober."

There had been similar reprimands and negative evaluations in his career, which it pained him to remember, as though he were tearing off his own mask. He then upbraided himself with vile words and drank more heavily, but it seemed that consciousness could not be dispelled, no matter how deep he drank. A blaze remained which could not be extinguished.

32

"I am unreliable," so ended the monologue. A man reproaches himself with failure in the very thing he values most. The cuirassiers are reliable; thus Goldhammer thought back most fondly to the days when he had served with them.

The Rhenish Cuirassier Regiment Count Gessler was stationed in Deutz; its commander was the Prince of Wales. The sturdy horsemen in the white uniforms were known

affectionately among the people as the Deutz "flour sacks."
When the barracks gates were opened after duty, women
and girls would crowd in front of them, also older,
well-dressed gentlemen. On Shrove Monday the first
squadron escorted the Carnival Prince. The staff trumpeter,
who on Sundays would stand in uniform on the Drachen-
fels and blow his trumpet, was known to every child in
Cologne. How often had Goldhammer heard him there
while looking down upon the Rhine, and treated him to a
bottle for playing a request. How time passed.

For requests the usual tip was a bottle of champagne. The
Rhinelanders are freehanded. Even then he was drinking,
but there was still something behind it: reliability.

A sense of euphoria came over him: "Among all the
regiments of Christendom, even those on horseback, we
cuirassiers are the only and the last in whom chivalry is still
alive. It will perish with us. We still wear armor and make
up the bodyguard."

This is how Goldhammer would cheer himself up when
he sat drinking in the Rue du Cherche-Midi. He had put
on his comfortable litevka; a fire was already burning in the
fireplace. The evenings were growing cooler; as it was, he
easily felt the chill.

The Deutzers had not seen action at Mars-la-Tour, but
the lucky coincidence of a transfer had allowed him to ride
in this famous attack—this memory surpassed all the others,
even that of his first love, which had been unhappy.

"There's only one other thing I would wish for: that I
had fallen that day—shot off my horse like Marées or
pierced by a lance like so many all around."

He poured himself a drink and sighed: "Strange that with all my ideals I always think of death, as though it made them even more exalted. It was precisely my love for Dorothea that made her unattainable; my adoration had put her out of reach. But even when I hadn't yet realized this I thought of death. I seem to sense in it a higher intensity; what's more, my concept of sovereignty includes suicide. In fact, it is the ultimate sovereign act, next to tears and laughter, the human monopoly."

He poured himself another glass and laughed: "A fine cuirassier! I'm an out-and-out failure. And thoroughly incapable of making use of my sovereignty, too craven even to walk across the street. It's written all over my face. Lackey of my own thoughts, which have neither justice nor conviction behind them. I'm one of those who cries his heart out to prostitutes."

Once he had had a good memory; he had known every man in his squadron by name. Now he mixed up names and dates; when leafing through his memory he would confuse the pages. Marées, also one of the Deutzers, had not fallen at Mars-la-Tour, but the following winter at Sapignies. In fact, Goldhammer had often enough joined in the song:

"Whenever we relive it, the fourth of January . . ."

During his command he had had to report directly to Schwartzkoppen, the division commander, and had made a good impression on him. The general's son, his present chief, had remembered this when he recruited him. But one could not speak of protection. An aide with military and legal experience was virtually a windfall for a military attaché. But Goldhammer had to admit that right at the beginning he had failed in a delicate mission. Gradually his responsibilities were reduced. Now he sat in the outer office clipping newspaper articles. Whenever a visitor could not find his way, he had to show him the door and also announce him. In other words, a glorified doorman. But now that, too, was more than he could handle. Even the orderlies scarcely took notice of him.

Here one might illuminate yet a third character of Goldhammer's: his highly sensitive and sentimental nature, in which the actual reason for his drinking was to be found. He failed precisely because he took things too seriously which he was thoroughly equal to physically and mentally.

Indeed, the sentimentality of this iron knight was extraordinary. Its symptoms had claimed the attention of doctors—thus a curious report appears in Steckel, which he had heard from colleagues in Bonn, in connection with this patient.

The encounter with Dorothea had been a *Voyage autour de ma chambre*: a novel which had taken place solely in Goldhammer's imagination. It had culminated in a disorder—a muteness, an inability to speak which had lasted for almost a month. A disfunction of this kind often follows in the wake of a violent emotion—expressions like "I'm at a loss for words" or "that leaves me speechless" are indicative of this. It was the duration here that seemed so unusual; the psychiatrists even began to worry that the illness was incurable. They identified it as a purely emotional disturbance—the patient's behavior was like that of a bird that hops and flies like all the others, but no longer sings.

Goldhammer's third character, the sentimental one, may explain why Gerhard hit upon him as a second. He was one of the few Gerhard had really noticed and of whom he had retained more than just name and rank. Goldhammer, too, had taken a liking to the boy at first sight—perhaps he sensed a kinship between them: the feeling of not belonging to a society that one was part of. The one was not taken seriously intellectually, the other morally, although both were still tolerated. They discovered each other, as it were, like two loafers, and even though they rarely spoke, they were often seen together.

Gerhard felt: this friend—he did not dare call him that—meant well by him. That is why he had given his name as second. To be sure, this choice could not possibly have fallen upon anyone less apt than the Rittmeister.

33

Heinrich had already cautiously opened the door several times; today the Rittmeister was sleeping even longer than usual—he had not been to work for days.

"Sleeping" was perhaps not the right word; it was rather a prolonged stupor with interruptions. Just to get on his feet Goldhammer needed a cognac; the bottle which he drank from all day stood on the night table next to his bed. The master often left the mail unopened for days at a time; instead he would leaf through books and newspapers which he then threw on the floor. It could happen that he would sit down at the piano; he played marches and other things that appealed less to Heinrich, and sometimes just a muddle of noise as if hail were beating down on the keys.

Heinrich was saddened by the growing disorder. His master lived more like a student or a gypsy than a soldier. The orderlies sent by the Attaché had to go back without an answer. Things had gotten serious; they would surely end badly—but just how, the loyal soul could not imagine. In his eyes the Rittmeister had something invulnerable. He was a baron—to deprive him of even a trace of respect would be improper for a servant. He loved the Rittmeister. He had ridden next to him at Mars-la-Tour and had covered his left flank. Both wore the Iron Cross—Heinrich on a ribbon, the Rittmeister on his chest.

Now the master was ill, and Heinrich suffered with him as if he himself were ill—the malady was indeterminate and difficult to explain, as many illnesses are. Who could tell the cause? Heinrich did not say: "The master drinks," but: "He isn't feeling well," and when he turned away the orderlies, not: "He's still in bed," but rather: "He has business in the city."

Goldhammer gave a start when Heinrich came in and announced a visitor. Just before that the sound of voices had disturbed him.

"There is a strange officer outside who insists on speaking to the Herrn Rittmeister."

"Tell him to go to hell and you leave me alone!"

"It's a man from the Navy, he says that he's come in an affair of honor. He says it's urgent, Herr zum Busche sent him. He's waiting in the hall."

"Affair of honor"—even in his dissoluteness this affected Goldhammer as if someone had grabbed his porte-épée. His young friend's name did the rest. What he could have to do with this was, of course, a mystery to the Rittmeister. Perhaps he only needed some advice—in any case, he wasn't to have thought of him in vain. He rose to his feet:

"Heinz, open the curtains and show the gentleman into the drawing room. Please tell him to be patient for a moment."

He reached for the bottle of cognac and pushed it away again. "I should really shave—I'll excuse myself on account of illness. But at least I might appear in uniform."

He put on his litevka, then trousers and boots, and went into the drawing room where Mauclerc was waiting for him, who, though retired for a number of years, had changed from his hunting coat back into uniform. Goldhammer remembered, as he greeted the officer, that he knew him and had once even sat next to him at the Crillon. This shortened the introduction. Mauclerc came right to the point, which was indeed urgent and suffered no delay.

It was no trifling matter. The role Gerhard was said to have played in it seemed to the Rittmeister at first implausible—an adventure like the one in the "Golden

Bell" he might have expected of anyone but this naive admirer from a distance. And then, even more incredible: with a married woman. But Mauclerc gave his word that Gerhard had admitted his guilt, even his role as the seducer. Without a doubt, Kargané had a right to any form of satisfaction he wished, and his second had come to him, the Rittmeister, in order to arrange a time and place for the encounter. Here it could only be pistols, and at short range.

So a duel with pistols was to be negotiated—or, as the Rittmeister preferred to call it, a bout with pistols. In the Bonn Corps, whose colors he had worn, the pistol was considered a weapon of inferior rank, and more often than not very little came of the farce. Old gentlemen with young wives might get away with pistols, but the active man preferred the blade.

Both seconds had experience in this matter, which they settled point by point without any real disagreements. Given the short notice, they had to choose a place as close by as possible—the best being the Old Mill not far from the Fort Montrouge. It was abandoned and known to initiates as the classic place for such encounters. Only the granary was in good condition, where the peasants had once garnered their wheat; after the construction of the fort it had served the garrison as a drill ground in bad weather. Now it stood empty, apart from the meetings which had become more frequent lately. The political climate had grown ruder, and journalists went there to inflict on each other a scratch or two.

There was a great advantage in the covered loft; it

shielded the place of combat from the eyes of curious passers-by, above all, from reporters. The physician, Doctor Mandel, lived right nearby, at the Porte d'Orleans. A brief message would suffice—he then took his top hat down from its peg; it was a morning stroll for him. He did not carry a bag, because in the Old Mill there was a wall cupboard that contained the necessities: bandages, ether, instruments for minor surgery.

Also among those in the know was Krumbach, a coachman who had come from Alsace after the war. Krumbach was reliable; they had given him the nickname "Père Charon." He drove a carriage and pair, and for years had had a kind of monopoly on the trips to the Old Mill, which yielded a good tip as well. His horses could have found the way in their sleep, even before daybreak.

The tip was often handsome, because most of his customers climbed in for the ride back with an elation as if they had won at the lottery. That Krumbach also delivered passengers to the morgue was probably a predictable phantasy. Hence the nickname.

In any case, it was to the old man's advantage that he had his stand on Montparnasse. He was engaged for these trips when it was still dark in the city, and he arrived at the Old Mill at sunrise. This was impossible tomorrow; there was still much to do. So they agreed on eleven o'clock sharp—an unusual time.

The only contention arose with regard to the distance. As with the other details, Kargané had left this to the discretion of his second, who considered twelve paces appropriate.

The Rittmeister was opposed to this—double the number was quite sufficient. Mauclerc would hear nothing of this.

"Herr von Goldhammer—you know as well as I do that tomorrow they won't be shooting into the air. The grievousness of the insult rules that out, in fact prohibits it. The encounter should therefore be as brief as possible."

Essentially, that was also the Rittmeister's view. It was the language he understood. But a duel, after all, is not an execution. That would also be detrimental to Monsieur de Kargané's reputation.

So they agreed on fifteen paces.

34

The Rittmeister came back late to his apartment. He had shaved and for the first time in a long while felt good about himself again. Perhaps what really mattered was that a person, whatever his moral outlook, was at one with himself. Then the other things harmonized as well. They had fallen into place practically without effort; one link of the chain fit into the other. Heinrich had found Krumbach at his stand; the coach would be punctually at hand. He now arranged his things for the following morning. Uniform was out of the question for the Rittmeister; he had made it a condition that the other side also dispense with it. But they would wear their decorations.

The referee had also been found with no trouble—a

retired colonial, Commandant Marteau. The Rittmeister would have preferred someone neutral, but after all, in matters like this, good blood was more important even than skin color. It could also have been a yellow man, but then a Samurai. Besides, there was hardly a choice. Marteau lived right around the corner on the Boulevard Raspail. Mauclerc had informed him of an important visit.

After the Rittmeister had freshened up, he went to meet Mauclerc in front of Marteau's house. Upstairs a native servant admitted them and announced their visit. The retired officer received them in his dressing gown; despite the time of year he sat shivering by the fire. "Pardon my slovenly appearance—today I've been living entirely on quinine." Although it was a large room, the trophies looked grotesque; they would have fit better in a museum of natural history.

The Rittmeister knew this slightly strained voice of the Old Gentlemen who insisted on tradition. "Tête blanche— queue verte"—a favorite saying of Gallifet's. Old roosters, but when they got going their crests would swell.

And likewise here. When the Commandant heard them speak of pistols and the role intended for him, he grew animated and of course accepted—the more readily as the young Prussian was involved, who had once made an unfavorable impression on him. This might be a chance to contribute to the "Revenge for Sadowa." What had happened in the meantime he had missed in Tonkin or on Madagascar.

The Commandant agreed to everything the seconds had

arranged; they were able to leave after a half hour. When they had risen to go, he added: "You surely do not expect me beforehand to propose an amicable settlement. That would be as superfluous as it is inappropriate." They agreed.

The visit to Gerhard zum Busche was a personal need for the Rittmeister, not merely an unavoidable duty. To his astonishment he did not find his young friend bewildered as he had feared, but in a tranquil mood, almost cheerful. Gerhard thanked him cordially and apologized for the trouble he had put him to, but at the same time requested that they dispense with a discussion—somewhat like a patient who is loath to hear the details of an unavoidable operation. The Rittmeister had said: "You needn't worry about a thing—I'll pick you up. I have only one request: that you really shoot at him, and not just in the air."

In this respect his mind was at ease: Gerhard would not cut a poor figure. Perhaps there would be a miracle. But the more he brooded, the more apprehensive he became. The Captain was known as one of the best shots. Goldhammer imagined how after the signal he would nonchalantly raise his pistol and without aiming pull the trigger. He would shoot the boy down like a pigeon.

Only one person would cut a pitiful figure in all this: I, the Rittmeister. I'm not in the right frame of mind; I can't take it. I have reported sick for a week—I shouldn't even go. That would be the height of infamy. After all, Kargané is in the right. The formalities are correct, and yet the whole thing is out of line. That must be my fault.

He thought it over again. Although he had sworn he

would stay sober, he poured himself a cognac. This one simply had to be the last, otherwise it could end up being a long night, as it had all week. During these phases Gold-hammer was never really sober; when he did not drink, his condition grew even more confused. A keener awareness brought nothing besides pain. Dealings with the outside world were impossible; he noticed that in conversation or even reading a report he became more and more confused, the more he tried to concentrate. In the morning hours he had attacks of anxiety that grew to the point of breathless-ness. He heard the murmuring of a crowd gathering in front of the house; they would pass judgment on him.

Like many in his situation, he had thought about suicide. Nothing seemed simpler, and yet it was incredible how the resistance grew when one held the pistol in his hand and had cocked the hammer—a slight pressure of the finger, just a touch, would have sufficed to enter Nirvana.

It would be good if someone could be found to take it off one's hands. The Rittmeister was no friend of the death penalty, just as any sort of attack on someone who could not defend himself was repugnant to him—but he made an exception with himself. To be executed, perhaps even innocently, was a fast and clean way to die, one which Caesar already had praised as the best.

"Perhaps after the word is given I should jump between them and cover the boy with my body—that would be his salvation and a good exit for me. I'm finished anyway. In any case, something's got to happen. In short—the duel must not take place. I'll report it to the police. The part of informer, that's the final touch: anonymously, and from a second as well. An affair of honor from beginning to end."

Goldhammer sat down at the secretary and arranged his writing material. He had crossed one leg over the other and was shocked when it began to swing like a pendulum. He had to hold it with his left hand. But he wrote fluently, as if receiving dictation. After he had closed and sealed the envelope without applying his signet, he rang the bell and roused Heinrich from his sleep.

"Heinz—an express letter for the Cité. Drop it off with the night watchman. Say it's urgent—but offer no explanations. I'm depending on you."

35

Etienne had not left the Palais until after midnight—when he came back the next morning Dobrowsky was still in his office. The man had to have a machine in his head. He had already dealt with visitors and was sitting at his desk in front of a pile of letters which Delavigne was opening and showing to him. Some of them had been brought in by the night watchman, others had been delivered along with the mail or by messengers. "Mostly dead wood" was the Inspector's comment—it was above all the large reward that had motivated many of them.

"Just this last one," said Dobrowsky to Delavigne, as his glance fell on a "Petit Bleu" with a red seal. "Then we'll call it a day; maybe we can catch a bit of sleep until noon. Anyway, the case is clear."

Etienne had not yet recovered from his astonishment when he saw his friend's face go rigid as soon as he had run through the letter. The Inspector asked for a street map and looked at the clock. Then he jumped up.

"That's all we needed. Delavigne, rush over to the fire station! I'm requisitioning the fastest wagon along with its crew. Tell them to hitch up—no matter where else there's a fire."

Meanwhile in the Old Mill preparations were being made for the duel; except for Gerhard, everyone was familiar with the protocol. The room was bright; it had once been used for cultivating silkworms.

The door was closed; it was guarded by Heinrich and the Count's coachman. Kargané's carriage and Père Charon's were standing in front of it. Even Doctor Mandel had not come on foot today—from all he had heard, there could be more for him to do on the premises than usual. His cupboard was open; the instruments were lying spread out on the little table in front of it. After the formal greeting the Rittmeister had measured off the distance—with the greatest bounds he could manage. The weapons were loaded and checked. The adversaries had removed their jackets. After the referee had announced the conditions in his sharp voice, he concluded:

"I now request the gentlemen to choose their weapons and take their positions. I shall count to three. Monsieur de Kargané has the first shot."

There was a silence. Gerhard and Kargané stood facing each other; the sun fell through the skylight. The Rittmeister had trouble staying on his feet; the bounds had exhausted him. He thought: it's too bright. Their shirts are as white as targets. If the boy would at least stand sideways— — —

The moment the Commandant raised his arm and was about to start counting, he was interrupted by an unusual sound: a ringing of bells or rather a shrill clanging that was rapidly drawing nearer. The Rittmeister, who trusted his senses less and less, thought he was hearing things. Surely it was the blood pounding in his temples. Or would there be a miracle after all?

The clanging stopped. Right after that the door was burst open—with such force that its panels fell into the room. A little man in a dark suit rushed in, followed by men in uniform with axes in their hands. It was Dobrowsky, deus ex machina.

"In the name of the law; everyone stay where they are. Gentlemen, put down your weapons!"

Gerhard, who was standing facing the door, saw it disappear as if a stage curtain were being raised; outside, horses whinnied, men in Greek helmets were coming toward him. He fell to the ground: "I've been hit, it's beautiful—more beautiful than I thought."

Goldhammer felt relieved of a great burden. Truly a miracle, almost a resurrection. Mauclerc, across from him, was glaring at him contemptuously. "The Captain has been denounced. It could only have been this degenerate agent;

I knew he couldn't be trusted the minute I set eyes on him. I'll pay him back for this. A challenge is out of the question, but from now on nobody will have anything more to do with him, much less a gentleman give him his hand."

Kargané had been standing with his back to the door, next to the doctor's table; he laid his pistol down on it. The Inspector, accompanied by Etienne, walked up behind him. He said in a low voice:

"Monsieur de Kargané, I was just able to stop you at the last moment from committing a second murder. The victim of the first was the dancer, whom you mistook for your wife. You've been under observation. I'll have to take you before the examining magistrate. Follow me without a row. But don't touch that pistol!"

The warning came too late, as did Dobrowsky's hand reaching for the weapon. Kargané had seized it and aimed it at himself—Etienne, who wanted to snatch it from him, also was too late.

Doctor Mandel was on the spot as the blood was still spreading over the Captain's silk shirt. He knelt down beside him and immediately stood up again: "This man is beyond help—the shot was fatal."

"It was his best," added the Inspector. "I'd like to have a few words with you before you write out the death certificate."

The doctor said: "Right now I must attend to the young gentleman—he needs me now. And Herr von Goldhammer isn't feeling well either."

A combination of murder and suicide, as the Rittmeister

had foreboded the night before. But he had been thinking of Gerhard. As often with premonitions the frame had been accurate, but the cunning with which it had been filled had come as a surprise. That was uncanny.

By midday the "Old Mill" already stood empty again; protagonists and extras in the drama had dispersed. The first to leave were the firemen; they were used to baneful scenes. Père Charon drove the dead Captain to the morgue, Mauclerc accompanied him. For the present, Doctor Mandel wanted to bring Gerhard to his office; there he would examine him further. The Rittmeister was with him; the Inspector had also assigned Delavigne to go along.

"You're responsible to me that nothing foolish happens on the way!"

Dobrowsky had no choice but to requisition Kargané's hunting carriage. He rode back with Etienne, who, no sooner had he gotten in, sank into an insuperable daze. The spell did not pass until the coach stopped in front of his apartment and the Inspector shook him out of it. The events in the mill had swept over him like a storm; he was so confused and exhausted that he had not even asked the Inspector a question. Dobrowsky patted him on the shoulder:

"Dear friend, you've got to get some rest. I still have a long afternoon ahead of me. The mountain has been climbed, but the descent can be treacherous, too—we'll soon find out. I expect you at eight o'clock at our table in the "Four Sergeants"—"to beat the bowls," as an old huntsman like Kargané would have said."

EPILOGUE

36

Etienne found the Inspector at the usual place. His friend
was in a strange mood—half animated, half distracted. He
was in excellent spirits and so talkative that he often lost the
thread. He chewed nervously on his lips; his pupils were
unusually large. New was also the little red ribbon he was
wearing in his buttonhole.

"Inspector—I admire you. Compared to you, Sherlock
Holmes is a beginner."

Dobrowsky waved off the compliment: "I was lucky.
Don't forget all the help I was given. Of course, delegating
is also an art—I can take credit for that. And without
cocaine it wouldn't have been possible; I can still feel its
effects."

They saw Leprince go past, behind him a lady wearing an
autumn fur. The Inspector followed them with his eyes.
"Look—a new one. He saw us, but didn't say hello. I'm
afraid I'll soon be having to deal with him."

Etienne did not know where to begin. "First of all, my
congratulations. I see the reward was quick in coming. You
truly earned it."

Again the Inspector waved it off: "Things are not as
simple as you suppose. My achievement, if you want to call
it that, was not so much that I solved the case, but that

unnecessary to-do was avoided in the process and will continue to be avoided."

"So it's a form of hush money?"

"No, no. You mustn't think of it that way. Rather as appreciation for the fact that the police do not overstep their bounds. It is not up to them to decide whether a case is closed or not. They supply facts, retrieve them. To exploit a case politically or to judge it morally is not their duty. Apparently it's better that this case be left pending. Besides, we still lack conclusive evidence. Kargané shot himself, but didn't make a confession."

The Inspector ordered drinks and in passing questioned the waiter about Leprince's companion. Then, after he had tasted and approved the wine:

"Etienne—it would be wrong of you to take me for a Macchiavelli, but without a pinch of that we wouldn't get anywhere. The Minister doesn't demand strict obedience; he's broad-minded. He was even pleased that I requisitioned the fire brigade. That exceeded my authority; I had no right to do it. But it was a matter of seconds. Otherwise zum Busche would no longer be alive."

Etienne found Dobrowsky a bit too nonchalant, like someone who knows a lot more than he is saying. He pushed the point:

"Inspector—I'm still baffled. Do you mean to say when you accused Kargané to his face of the murder you were just beating the bushes? And you had the luck to have just what you were expecting jump out?"

The Inspector shook his head. "There was no doubt in

my mind that he was the one, and between you and me, there still isn't—what astonished me was only his split-second reaction to my accusation. He realized immediately that I would get him in the long run—he shortened the procedure and thus did us a favor. When I saw him go for the pistol, I was afraid he would try to kill zum Busche anyway—but he was too intelligent for that. The boy's death would have fit the role of the cuckolded husband—but that was played out. It would be underestimating the Captain to think him capable of jealousy. The young man was indifferent to him—I even think it possible that he liked him."

Dobrowsky repeated: "The fact is—I was lucky. I don't pretend to be clairvoyant—but the man with the handkerchief turned up just as I foretold. And he's exactly as I imagined him: an ensign in the Navy, seventeen years old, on a week's leave in Paris. His ship is anchored outside Toulon. A charming lad, very much the dancer's taste. He came to the office after midnight in order to protest his innocence, which I never doubted.

"Now listen to this: I managed to get out of him that he ran into Kargané on the backstairs right before the murder. He could swear to it—everyone in the Navy knows the Captain. I repeat, I was already onto him, the very moment I learned of the mix-up with the rooms. But what do I mean 'mix-up'—both women are very similar in taste and temperament, also in their choice of lovers. And then the same situation—not only in place and time—it's no wonder that even the Captain was deceived.

"But one thing at a time; I want you to see the whole picture. There are still blank spaces—but also conjectures that fill them."

Dobrowsky, as was his way, proceeded from the general to the particular. First: what has to be considered when a woman is murdered? It can happen for reasons that have nothing to do with sex. The woman is just in the way, or someone is out to rob her. But if sex enters into it, one can infer jealousy, revenge, infidelity, or simply an inexplicable hatred directed against everything feminine. In the first case, a specific woman will be the victim, in the second, any one at all.

In the latter case, the murder in the "Golden Bell" could be the beginning of a series of crimes. Then the dancer would have been the victim of a terrible coincidence. That makes the investigation more difficult, as they found out in London; it fans out into the indeterminate. But if the dancer was singled out as a person, then the murderer had to be sought among her acquaintances. A great many were listed in her red notebook; there would be a lot of work and trouble, but hardly results.

The picture changed when the Inspector learned of the confusion of suites. What if the Countess had been meant personally? Then the Count's name immediately came to mind.

Dobrowsky recapitulated what had happened since noon the day before yesterday: Gerhard's encounter with Irene, the still unclear role that Ducasse had played in it, the violent quarrel between the Karganés, Gerhard's bouquet of roses, the Countess's note—whether it was thanks or in fact an invitation. Kargané, still seething with rage, had watched the messenger, perhaps even demanded that he be given the note to read. Whatever the case—he knew what was in store that evening; he knew the time and the place. It was not the first time he had suffered this affront. Moreover, it was possible that Irene had thrown her intentions in his face—she was capable of that. Kargané himself was known in the "Golden Bell"; it was even said that he numbered among the initiates who had a key to the service entrance—which, if it was true, had not been necessary that evening. Whatever the case—he had been right there like a hunter in his stand after sighting his game.

His marriage had long been a burden to him; he wanted to be rid of the woman. The scene in the afternoon had been the last straw. Now his mind was made up. At the same time he thought up an alibi. He had ordered his carriage to drive to the club. Instead of that he gave Mauclerc instructions for the hunting party and had the charabanc hitched up. The Inspector had managed to learn this much from Kargané's driver during the ride back from the Old Mill, but the coachman, also a Breton, suddenly fell silent. Whether the Captain had really gone hunting, for which there would have been ample time, Dobrowsky left open for now. He had been seen with Mauclerc in the carriage that morning—that sufficed for an alibi.

Probably he had lurked in the fog behind the Madeleine

until Irene had gotten out of the carriage, thus dispelling the last of his doubts. Before that the dancer had arrived with her ensign; Bourdin had offered them suite number Twelve. She had done so in the hope of making a small profit—fortunately for the Countess, unfortunately for the dancer.

Meanwhile della Rosa had made herself comfortable with her ensign, like Irene and Gerhard, who came shortly afterwards. The Inspector repeated: "Two young men on their first adventure—a strange coincidence, but not so unusual in this place."

He turned to Etienne: "We've surely all had similar experiences. The ensign grew more and more anxious, the more the rose shed its leaves. I don't mean to be cynical— the mystery the Vestals preside over is tremendous—and, although it wasn't her due, it was precisely this effect that the dancer sought and enjoyed."

The young man got scared. He threw open the door and rushed out into the corridor. In the half-dark he lost track of the way he had come. He found the back stairs, which were lit up by a gas flame. On the landing he stopped for a moment to collect his thoughts, perhaps even to turn around and go back—then he heard footsteps coming up the stairs. He pressed himself into a niche and got a glimpse of Kargané, who walked past without seeing him.

"That dispelled my last doubts. Sure enough I was on the right track—when I heard about the mix-up of rooms I became suspicious. Here it wasn't just any woman that had to die, but a specific one."

Why would the Captain peer into the next room before committing the murder? Perhaps as a precaution, perhaps he himself did not know why. At any rate, when he struck, he thought he was in front of the right door. He didn't even have to open it, because the dancer had seen to that. No doubt she had expected that the ensign would come back. She had probably heard noise coming from next door and was standing scantily dressed in the doorway. Kargané could only make out her silhouette, since the suite was lit up and the corridor almost dark. The women were the same size and above all—the man was a beast of prey—had the same scent.

Here the Inspector could not help praising Delavigne—he had done some good investigating. "Chant de Châtaigne" came as a distillate of chestnut blossoms from the Far East and was unknown to the large firms. A dealer in the Rue du Bac imported it for a small clientele. Delavigne had gone over his list.

The Captain must only have realized his mistake when he heard the dancer's voice: "Let go of me!" But then it was too late—the blow had been struck. Now it was *woman*—whether his own wife or any other. They began to merge—as did the men, thus Jack the Sailor and Kargané the Captain. And that both used a knife was no coincidence. Certainly it would have been easier for the Captain to use poison or simulate an accident.

The Inspector began to stray into generalities: "I never cease to be amazed at the amount of intelligence that is wasted on a crime. The effort stands in no relation to the risk. As in this case: Kargané held all the cards: proven adultery, divorce, a few shots in the air. Lombroso is right: crime is an evil endowment, a birth defect. Incidentally, I don't believe that the Captain was imitating the London monster. A man to whom everything is allowed doesn't need models. I'm told this is the motto that appears above the entrance to his hunting lodge. The Countess had her reasons for not going there."

He beckoned the waiter. "How about another drink— it's incredible how lively I feel; to think I was rushing around all afternoon. But a little ribbon like this is not bad, although people make fun of it. I even wore it on my coat, and a policeman who didn't know me escorted me across the street—*un monsieur décoré*.

As a matter of fact, he had hardly even found time to roll a cigarette the entire day. The rumor about what had happened in the Old Mill had reached the Cité well ahead of him. The fire brigade had seen to that. After he had taken Etienne home, the Inspector had immediately been summoned to the prefect and from there sent to the Minister. After that he had drawn up the death certificate with Doctor Mandel. "Accident while unloading a weapon" was the best formula that offered itself—everyone agreed. Even the Inspector had to admit that it might have happened that way after he had startled the Captain with his warning.

And could he maintain with absolute certainty that Kargané was the murderer? Surely there were sound reasons for thinking so, but proving it would have required lengthy investigations. As it was, the alibi for the night of the murder was difficult to refute—these Bretons like Mauclerc and the coachman, the ensign, too, had a different sense of justice; they were sharpshooters who vouched for each other to the point of perjury.

Certainly there was convincing evidence—but was it enough for a conviction? However meticulously one fitted it together—it remained a house of cards. Maître Demange, whom Kargané would undoubtedly have engaged, would blow it down.

But what was the point? Kargané was dead. As the Inspector had heard from Paturon, they were preparing an elaborate funeral for him. Inquiries would bring him needlessly back to life and cause harm on all sides. Neither the widow nor her lover, nor the guests of the "Golden Bell" would be helped by it—quite the contrary. The Admiral, as father-in-law, was already receiving visits of condolence; he had put on mourning. Above all, the Navy—*le drapeau*.

The case was closed or about to be closed as far as Kargané was concerned. Here the Inspector had agreed with the Minister. All that remained unsatisfied was the instinct of the hunting dog on a fresh scent just before the quarry. But what was the use of bringing in game that was not welcome? Policemen who continue an investigation on their own can only reap ingratitude—there were examples enough of this. That was *l 'art pour l 'art* or a job for paid detectives and for journalists.

Dobrowsky patted the ribbon: "The dossier is closed; the case remains unsolved. I'm afraid, for our colleagues in London it will not be any different."

Wilflingen, January 30, 1984.

About the Author

Ernst Jünger was born in Germany in 1895. At seventeen he joined the foreign legion and later fought in World War I. His war experiences were recounted in his memoirs *Storms of Steel*. A captain in Worls War II, Jünger took part in the occupation of France. *On the Marble Cliffs*, his allegorical anti-Nazi novel, was published in 1939 and became an international bestseller. Jünger lives in the Swabian Highlands, and devotes his life to writing and entomology. Among his other works are *Paris Diaries*, *The Worker* and *The Glass Bees*. Marsilio has published the novel *Aladdin's Problem*, and will publish *Eumeswil* and *Heliopolis*.

The Eridanos Library